OREGON OBSESSION

ROMANCE ACROSS STATE LINES

DEBBIE WHITE

CHAPTER 1

*L*iving alone took some getting used to. Dealing
with the pain and sorrow of losing someone to
a tragic event such as the terrorist attack on the
Twin Towers, Maggie knew all too well the anguish and
sadness that came with such a harrowing experience.
She remembered the day clearly as so many Americans
did.

She was sitting on her couch, putting on her tennis
shoes to go for her walk when an emergency announcement broke through the daily show. She moved to the
edge of her seat to get a better glimpse of what was
happening. Shaking her head uncontrollably, she began
to cry. Richard's office was in one of the buildings. He
was senior partner at a very prestigious law firm.

With her pulse racing, she grabbed for the phone

and dialed Richard's number. The line beeped nonstop. She clutched her chest and cried out. *Noooo!* With her worst fears realized, she slumped to the floor. *Collette. My sweet girl, Collette. How am I going to tell her?*

Over the course of the next several weeks, Maggie walked around in a state of shock. She vaguely recalled getting through it all. So many memorials to attend, so many to comfort. She found it difficult to go into the city any longer. She sheltered Collette and became so overprotective she began to smother her. When one of her closest friends, who'd since moved away to another state, came for a visit and began to tell her about her new life in Oregon, Maggie took notice. A new start in a new state could be what would help them move on. So on the invitation of an old friend, Maggie and Collette left New York for peaceful Eugene, Oregon. And she never looked back.

~

When the realtor took her down the narrow two-lane road, Maggie wasn't sure about the location. So far off the beaten path. But when he showed her the small house with a national park nearby, she fell in love with the simplistic yet cozy feeling of the home and the area.

She and Collette would explore the trails later, enjoying a nice lunch under one of the many trees at the park. Because of its location, it wasn't busy most of the time. Unless it was someone on a hunt for a covered bridge that is.

Deep in the woods, about three miles or so, stood a covered bridge. Back in the day it probably saw a lot of action, but due to lack of funds, the poor bridge had seen better days. And because it wasn't on anyone's radar, it was a hit or miss when someone came to the park and also discovered the bridge.

Maggie kind of liked the solitude in the beginning. But as with anything else, as time marched on, her taste changed too.

Maggie was at a crossroads like this now.

In the beginning, Collette needed her mother, and more than ever the duo formed a bond that no one could tear apart. But when Collette began college it wasn't long after that she met Jeremy. Soon she was spending time with her new boyfriend, and it was during those lonely evenings Maggie's mind would drift. Sometimes to places better left untraveled, undiscovered, packed deeply, maybe never to be explored.

After Collette married and moved out, Maggie had to come to grips with the fact she was all alone. Many nights she cuddled up on the couch, crying herself to sleep. Left with only the sounds of silence, all those feelings came crashing in. She kept busy, but the truth was, she was lonely. Very lonely.

When they first came to Eugene, Maggie worked for an insurance company. It was more about keeping busy than needing money. She'd been the beneficiary of a large settlement with Richard's death. But the days were long, especially while Collette was attending school. After she graduated and went to college, not only were the days long but so were the evenings and weekends.

Katherine set her up on a few dates, and for the most part, the company was appreciated, and it did one thing if nothing else. Kept her busy and therefore not always focused on Richard and why this had happened.

Not that any person can ever replace a true love, but Maggie found so many things wrong at every level with her dates. They didn't have a chance of getting anywhere with her, let alone a second date.

Katherine finally got the message and stopped fixing her up. She fell back in love with reading, gardening, and long walks.

With several years behind her, she was getting a little older, fully retired and not enjoying living alone. She began to feel the emptiness and wondered why on earth she couldn't have seen this coming.

*H*iking seemed to clear the cobwebs, rejuvenate her soul, and with the holidays just around the corner, keep her weight down. Now that she was sixty, all she had to do was look at a sugary sweet and the pounds jumped on her, going right to her hips. Her plans for the day were to go grocery shopping, a task she detested, and go on a nice hike. With the park across the way, she had her choice of a mild hike to the bridge or a more moderate one a few miles beyond. She felt like she needed the longer one today.

She stood at the sink rinsing out her bowl and spoon when she got a glimpse of a man at the park across the way. He sat on a collapsible canvas stool in front of an easel, and every now and then he'd look toward the creek. She couldn't see exactly what he was painting, but him sitting all alone made her wonder about him.

It was a beautiful fall day, and many of the trees still had leaves—although with each gust of wind more tumbled to the ground. Piles of dried leaves cluttered the ground, and in the distance, the blue cloudless sky gave the illusion it was a warm day.

She finished rinsing her dishes and set them in the drainer to dry. Living alone made kitchen cleanup almost painless. She crossed over to the pantry and did a quick survey of goods. Three cans of chicken noodle left, couple cans of chili along with a new package of chocolate chip cookies. She ran her hand along the boxes of tea. She still had plenty, and she still had a box of her favorite Italian blend coffee pods. She opened the refrigerator and did an inventory of the milk, half and half, and butter. Shaking the cartons, she took a whiff. Wrinkling her nose, she made a mental note to grab some at the store.

When she peered back out toward the park, the man was gone. She shrugged, then went about her business of watering the houseplants. The dirt seemed to dry out more during the heater season. She filled her watering can and went to each plant, giving them a drink. When she finished that, she set off for the store.

The drive into town was an easy one. Hardly any traffic on her end, and it made it a breeze to get to the post office, store, her doctor, and anything else she needed. Her daughter Collette, along with her husband, Jeremy, and Maggie's sweet grandson, Sam, lived about five miles from her. They got together often, and with Thanksgiving just a few weeks away, she knew she'd better buy the ingredients for her famous pumpkin cheesecake.

After she finished the shopping, she checked her post office box for mail, afterward treating herself to a latte at the little coffee shop and a warmed cinnamon roll dripping with icing. She savored every bite. She'd normally bypass the dessert, but she also knew she'd walk it off later. Rationalizing the consumption of calories helped her to enjoy it more. After her last bite, she wiped her mouth with a napkin. Waving to the coffee shop owner with a backhanded motion, she bent over, slurping the last sips of coffee before tossing her garbage and rushing off.

Feeling tired from her trip into town and a bit drowsy from the sugar overload of the cinnamon roll, Maggie talked herself out of the hike. Besides rationalizing everything, she was great at talking herself out of doing things too. If she didn't want to do something, she just didn't do it. Shaking her head, partly disgusted she'd talked herself so easily out of the hike, she settled onto her overstuffed couch with a mug of her favorite Italian coffee to watch a mystery romance on the one channel she watched the most, the Hallmark Channel. They were gearing up for the holiday lineup of movies, and she made a mental note to remember to watch as many as she could.

After a light dinner of canned chili and a slice of white bread smothered in butter, Maggie headed off to her bedroom. She entered the bathroom adjacent and began to scrub her face and brush her teeth and her hair. She gasped. *Another gray hair!* She leaned in to get a closer look. "Yep, those little buggers," she said. She tried to pluck them but with absolutely no resolve. Disgusted that age was creeping in on her and there was nothing she could do to stop it, she climbed into bed with the one electronic device she owned, her Kindle, and began to read a few lines of her newest download before getting extremely drowsy and falling asleep.

Spontaneity and zeal for anything had all but dried up. Or so she thought. She had to admit the house walls seemed to be closing in on her more each day. Now that she was labeled a senior, a term she didn't relish, and was slowing down just a tad, she found more idle hours that needed filling. The man with the easel popped into her mind. Maybe she'd take up painting. No, how about photography? She hurried to the back bedroom and rummaged through the closet. She pulled out an old 35 mm camera. She eyed the antique-looking box, and feeling the weight of it in her hands, she frowned. No doubt there was something lighter available. So, on a whim, she drove to the camera store. Maybe that would put a little zest in her very boring life.

The clerk behind the counter was young and easy-going. He laughed at her "senior moment" jokes, and when she said she wanted a camera that even a child could operate, he tossed his head back and laughed so hard he snorted.

"Well I'm glad I'm entertaining you this morning." She shrugged, then lowered her gaze to the glass display case. "What about that one. It looks simple enough."

"That would be an okay choice, but this one is better." He leaned down and pulled out a camera and placed it on the counter. "This is basically a one-button camera. One button to focus and one button to take the picture. It comes with one lens that will be good for someone just learning, but you can upgrade the lenses later on as you get more comfortable."

Maggie picked up the camera and held it, feeling the weight in the palms of her hands. "It's pretty light-weight too. My old camera is cumbersome."

"They've come a long way. So, what do you think?" He crossed his arms and stepped back.

"I think I'll take it."

Happy with her purchase, she headed home. When

she drove onto the gravel driveway, she noticed the man at the park again. She parked her car and then did something she wouldn't normally do. She went over to say hello.

There was no surprising the gentleman; with every step, Maggie crunched leaves under her shoes. He rolled his neck her way.

She put up her hand and waved. "Hi, there."

He put down his brush and stood. "Hello."

She gazed at his blue T-shirt that snugly wrapped around his biceps and solid chest. Her gaze moved further down where she noticed the belt buckle and narrow waist and hips, and more muscular limbs—his thighs. Her gaze traveled back to his. "You came back. I saw you here yesterday," she said with a bit of hesitation in her voice.

He narrowed his eyes, then motioned toward her house. "I saw you the other day looking out your window. I hope you don't mind me being here. I just assumed"—he tipped his chin toward the open space of the park— "that this is a public park?"

She tossed her head back and laughed. "No, of course I don't mind. It's a beautiful park for anyone and everyone to enjoy. What are you painting?" She stepped toward the easel.

"Just the landscape. Trees and birds." He lowered

his head, and Maggie could see his cheeks flush with color.

"I didn't mean to embarrass you. I love your painting." She crossed her arms and tipped her chin. "Do you live around here?" *Now whose cheeks were blushed?* "I'm sorry. I shouldn't be so bold."

"No, it's okay. No, I don't live around here. I'm visiting from San Francisco." He motioned toward the camera around her neck. "Photography?"

"I just dabble. In fact, this is a new camera." She picked it up and focused him in. She peered around the lens, locking gazes with him. "Do you mind if I take your picture while painting?"

"Not at all." He turned and picked up his brush and dabbed some brown on the canvas.

Maggie clicked, then turned the camera and clicked again. "I have no idea what I'm doing, but the youngster at the shop said this was so easy a baby could do it. Not sure if that was a compliment or a crude comment?" She shook her head and laughed.

"I've never been to San Francisco before. It's on my bucket list," she said, admiring his artwork and changing the subject.

"It's a pretty city, but not as peaceful as here." He reached for his paintbrush.

"I won't keep you any longer. I just wanted to say hello." She began to walk backward.

He nodded, and the corners of his mouth drew up.

"If you get too cold, I have hot tea...and chicken noodle soup. Not the homemade kind but the canned kind." She stopped suddenly when she realized she was rambling on a bit.

"Thanks for the offer." He turned his back and began studying his canvas.

She left him quickly, crunching leaves all the way back to her house.

Once inside, she leaned up against the door. *I don't know what just came over me.* She covered her mouth to conceal her silliness. It wasn't like her to be so bold. Maybe Collette and Katherine were right. She'd been living alone too long, and now, she was going the complete opposite of the shut-in she'd become. Shaking off her silly move, she made her way into the kitchen. But she couldn't help herself. She peered out the window to watch the man with the strong arms, alluring senses, and calm voice paint—even if it was from a distance. *I need a walk. A long walk.* She made her way down the hall to her bedroom. She slipped on her treaded boots for hiking and put on a medium-weight hoodie. Then she headed out the door.

She waved to the man and in passing spoke. "Trails.

They're this way." She pointed toward the small bridge that crossed the tiny creek.

He nodded. "Enjoy," he said.

She was happy to get outside and walk off all her past indiscretions of food, but also her lack of caution regarding this stranger. *Maybe I need to get a dog!*

Maggie timed her walk, and when she'd been gone for about forty minutes, she headed back home. She hoped the quiet man, as she now called him, was gone, but when she stepped over the little bridge and saw that he was, a little pang of sadness hit her.

~

The quiet man with the strong hands came back two more times. Each time, she went outside and visited with him, and during the last time, she brought her own folding chair. She sat a little distance from him and in silence watched him paint. She'd never seen anything like it before. Sure, in galleries but up close and personal while it was being done, nope, and it was a sight to be seen. She folded her hands in her lap.

"You are so graceful with the brush. Do you find it hard to hold?"

"No, not at all. I had to get used to learning how to

control the flow of the paint. It's been very good for my therapy." He dipped his brush and began to speckle the tip of the brush on branches he'd painted.

"Therapy?"

"Yes. My therapist felt I needed something to channel my anger."

Anger. Did this mellow guy have anger issues? "I see. What are you angry about?"

The man put the brush down and turned slightly. "Mainly how I can't control certain things," he said in a lowered voice.

She pushed out a burst of air. "I hear you on that front. If I could have only controlled a few things in my lifetime." She lifted her brows and shrugged.

"Do you live out here all alone?" He never turned around, just kept painting.

Her pulse quickened as she thought the question over. Collette and Katherine both would be screaming at her right now.

"Yes, I do."

"Any family around?"

Yep, they would be screaming, jumping up and down and probably pulling their hair out. Don't answer him!

"My daughter, her husband, and my grandson live nearby." *Take that, you ax murderer.* She shook her head. "What about you? Any family here?"

"No family here. My folks live in New York."

"New York? I used to live there."

He quickly whirled around, eyeing her up and down. While still holding his brush, he presented a most winning smile that showed his front teeth. "Do you like Oregon better?"

"Lots better."

"I can see why." He continued painting.

"I guess I've bothered you enough for one day." She stood, collapsing her stool and hooking it through her arm.

"You weren't bothering me. I enjoyed talking to you."

She laughed. "Well, have a nice day." She turned and started walking back to her house.

"Anytime you want to come sit and talk is fine with me," he said.

Maggie studied the back of his head. *If he was an ax murderer, surely he would have made his move by now.* "Okay. I just might take you up on that."

After Maggie got inside, she bolted the door just because she could hear both Collette and Katherine in her brain, shouting for her to do so. She rushed to the kitchen window. He was still sitting right where she'd left him. He seemed nice enough, but something was definitely different about him. He was handsome, alone, seeking professional help, and painting at a park in Eugene, Oregon.

~

"Just checking in, Maggie. How are you?"

The voice on the other end was a familiar one to Maggie, and it was the reason she was in Eugene. "I'm great, Katherine. And you?"

"Getting ready for the mad rush of holidays. You're going over to Collette's, right?"

"Yes, me and my famous pumpkin cheesecake." She giggled.

"One of these days you all should come over here."

Maggie rested her head on the sofa back. Katherine had a huge home with windows from one end to the other and a view to die for. "That would be great. I'll mention it to Collette."

"I was thinking about having a holiday party. So you put the bug in her ear for me," Katherine said.

"Will do. Hey, listen, Katherine…have you ever just met someone and thought wow this person seems so familiar or like you feel this pull toward them so much you wonder why?"

"Okay, first of all, are we talking a person or are we talking a guy?"

Maggie counted to five under her breath. "A guy."

"Maggie Regan, are you dating someone? Because if you are, I think that's great."

"No, nothing like that, Katherine. But this guy keeps coming to the park across the way, and I can see him painting. So today I introduced myself. Well, actually I guess I never even told him my name, but I did invite him in for hot tea."

"Don't be inviting strange men in for tea, hot or otherwise, Maggie Regan. He could be wanted or something."

"I'll tell you what he could be wanted for. I don't normally drool over men, but this guy's body is so perfect, not to mention his sandy blond hair, deep blue eyes…like the ocean, and…"

"Whoa, girl. Hold up. You just described every housewife's dream."

"He was soft-spoken, and the way he held the paintbrush literally took my breath away. His movements were so precise and moved like liquid."

"Stop. You're making me shudder."

"I know. So that's why I invited him in."

"Maybe have Jeremy check him out first."

"No! I can't tell Collette her mother is gushing over some man that most likely is several years younger."

"Okay, now I'm just out and out shivering. Younger, too?"

"Not a speck of gray hair anywhere." She ran her hand down her dark locks, thinking about the silver streaks she saw in the mirror earlier.

Katherine sighed into the phone. "Call me when you see him next. I'll hurry right over, and between you and me giving him the third degree, we can find out if he's on the up-and-up."

"No, we're not going to do that. Please, Katherine. We can't act like some love-starved cradle robbers." Maggie howled into the phone, laughing at her own surmise of the situation.

"Well let me know how it all works out. I'm dying of curiosity."

"I do know he doesn't live here. He's from San Francisco."

"San Francisco? He might be gay. You better find out right away before you waste any more time on him."

Maggie furrowed her brows. "He might be, but either way, he's one hunk of a guy." She shrugged. "We probably shouldn't be stereotyping people from San Francisco."

"You're right. It just popped into my brain. That's

what happens when you turn sixty. You say stuff that just pops right into your head."

Maggie thought about her brief encounter with the painter. She'd never have done that in a million years in her youth. Katherine was right to a certain point. With age came bravery, sometimes seasoned with stupidity.

CHAPTER 2

Trey carefully tucked his easel away in the back of his rental car. As he lowered the trunk, he got a glimpse of the woman's house. He could see the small dwelling nestled among a group of trees and a cloud of smoke drifting out of her chimney. She no doubt was curled up on the sofa with a cup of tea. Not ready to do anything about this deep-seated feeling he had, he jumped into his car and drove back to his hotel. While driving, a song came on, and soon it reminded him of her. Not the mystery woman, but the woman he was going to marry. Before his world came tumbling down, shattering any hope for happiness. Ever.

He shook off the tears that tried to rear their emotional head, and after he willed them away, only then could he concentrate on living. It was tough. Every single day he was reminded somehow of Lacy.

He unloaded his car, and after a bite to eat, he watched a little television only to drift off to sleep while the show played in the background. When he woke, it was chilly in the room. He grabbed his arms and rubbed them. He turned up the thermostat and then took a long, hot shower before finally settling in bed for the night with a good book.

He'd just turned the page when his phone rang. It was his mother.

"Hey, Mom."

"Hi, Son. Just checking in on you. Haven't heard from you in a while."

He chuckled. "I'm fine. I'm in Oregon for a few more days. I love it here this time of year. The leaves are so pretty, the air crisp and clean, and well, it's just what I need every so often."

"I don't know how you manage to live in San Francisco. It's so busy." Her voice went from soft to stern.

"Mom, we've been over this a zillion times. New York is a busy town!" he shot back.

She sighed into the receiver.

"When are you and Pops going to come out to San Fran and visit?"

"I was just going to ask you the same thing."

"What? When were you going to come for a visit?" He was confused.

"No, silly. You coming home. Thanksgiving is in two weeks."

"I'm not feeling the holidays yet. Maybe another time."

"Trey Simmons. I know you've been through hell and back. So many New Yorkers have, but don't you think you've cleared your head long enough. It's been seventeen years. We miss you." Her voice was caring again.

"Mom, too many bad memories there. I just can't."

"Lacy's parents haven't heard from you in a long time either. I ran into Helen the other day. They asked about you."

Trey stared at the ceiling.

"Trey?"

"Yes, I'm here."

"I'll let you go for the evening. It's late here."

Trey removed the phone from his ear, locating the time. There was a three-hour time difference. "Why are you still up?"

"I couldn't sleep. I've been worried about you."

"Don't worry about me, Mom. I'm just fine."

He ended the call and closed his book. He couldn't manage to read another page after that phone conversation. He turned off the light. Just as he drifted off to sleep, a vision entered his mind. A beautiful woman with soft laugh lines and jet-black hair sprinkled with a few silver strands and warm brown eyes that could melt any icy heart. Maybe even his.

~

Secretly he'd hoped mystery woman would come out and say hello again. He had a tendency to seem a bit aloof or so he'd been told. He rather saw it as being observant. Since the accident, he'd had exactly three girlfriends, and none of them worked out. Maybe a brief rendezvous with an older woman who loved his painting would be enough to ease the loneliness he'd felt for the past seventeen years. He shook off the crazy idea and began to set up his easel.

He worked the latch, opening the large black box that held his paints and brushes, and scanned the area for his next victim. He spotted a bird sitting on a limb void of any leaves. He ran his hand along his scruffy chin and then took the tops off of a few colors and began dipping his brush.

He'd already had some of the painting done from the previous visits. The tree with the bird would complete his masterpiece. He chuckled at his choice of words. Masterpiece to who?

He briefly peered over his shoulder. The window was empty of smiling faces. He turned his attention back to his subject, the bird, and began painting. The corners of his mouth turned up when crunching leaves followed by short blasts of breath came up behind him.

"Hello, it's me again," a soft, sweet voice said.

Trey turned slightly in his chair. "I see. How are you?"

"Cold," she said, hugging her arms.

"Yes, it's a bit chilly today. I'm trying to finish this painting. I've been working on it for almost a week." Holding up the brush, he shrugged.

"Are you sure I can't convince you to come inside for a cup of tea?" She batted her long, dark lashes that emphasized her blue eyes.

He shook off the wave of goose bumps that tried to make their way up his arm. "Twist my arm," he said.

She turned and led the way back to her house.

He quickly capped his paints so they wouldn't dry out, then hurried behind her. When they got to the front porch, she opened the screen door and invited him in. Once inside the space, the coziness of the room warmed him right up. He made his way to the red brick fireplace and fanned his hands in front of dancing flames. The kitchen was just a stone's throw from the living room. The house was compact, and just being inside told him a lot about her.

"Trey," he yelled out. "My name is Trey Simmons." He could hear her filling the tea kettle.

"Nice to meet you, Trey. My name is Maggie Regan."

Trey watched her as she lit the gas burner and set the kettle on the flame. His gaze journeyed down her slim frame to her rounded hips. Her silhouette took his breath away.

"Have you lived here long?" he asked as he rubbed his hands together, enjoying the fire.

"About seventeen years."

"That's about the time I moved to San Francisco," he said.

She reached up to the cabinet and brought down two cups. He watched her put a tea bag in each cup, and when the kettle whistled, she topped off each mug with boiling water.

He moved from the fireplace and sat at the table with her. The green ceramic cup held the heat. He wrapped his cold hands around it before bringing it up to his lips. The scent of cinnamon and rose wafted through his nostrils. He drew in a taste.

"You must have been a young man when you moved to San Francisco."

He tipped his head. "About twenty-four or so."

He followed her gaze as it fell onto a small table holding framed photos.

"Your family?" he asked.

"Yes, that's my daughter Collette and her husband Jeremy and their son, Sam."

"Nice family. And the other one?" He motioned with his chin to the frame that held a picture a young couple in wedding attire.

"That's us many moons ago," she said, lighting up when she viewed the silver frame.

"You look like you were very happy. How long ago did he pass away?"

"Seventeen years ago."

"Seventeen years ago?" he repeated.

She slowly nodded.

"He looks like a wonderful man. I'm sure you had many happy moments together." He drew in another taste of the tea, then relaxed back in the chair.

"Yes, we did. And in one moment everything changed. My whole life as I once knew it, changed forever."

"That's kind of my story too. One minute I'm engaged to my best friend, planning a wedding, living the dream, and poof, all of it was gone in a hot minute." He noted the time on his watch. "I better get back to my painting. There's only so much daylight left. Thanks so much for the tea." He slid his chair back and stood.

"Anytime you want to come in and warm up just knock. I always have a fire going, and it just takes a minute to boil water for tea." She walked him to the door.

"Thanks again, Maggie."

He gave her a backhanded wave, then trotted back to the park where his easel, covered in a few red and gold-colored leaves stood. The bird long gone, Trey would have to finish it the best he could from memory. He detected Maggie's profile in the window. Was she watching him, too? He turned back toward his painting.

With every encounter the brush made with the canvas, Trey released some sort of pent-up desire to express his innermost feelings. He deepened the sky to a vibrant turquoise, he emphasized the green leaves with a heavier stroke, and when it came time to add a little something to the nearby babbling creek he'd been painstakingly painting for a couple of days, he combined white and black to make gray. The perfect hue for water rolling off the rocks.

With his hand resting on his chin, he sat back and admired his work. He grunted. *The bird. It needs some-*

thing. He gazed at the array of colors. He dipped his brush in brown, then added some black, then white. He swirled it around. Then he took a clean brush, and with just the tip, dipped it into his new custom color. He dabbled a little around the bird's face, down his wings, then smiling, laid the brush down.

While his painting dried, he took a long walk. Earlier, while he was setting up, he'd noted a footbridge across the small creek. He crossed the small creek and meandered down a path covered in rich dirt, fallen leaves, and twigs. A rustling sound stopped him dead in his tracks. A small lizard reared its head, then hopped up on a nearby rock, watching him carefully. He laughed then continued on his walk. The sun, hidden by all the trees, made the area feel dark and foreboding. Sort of like his mood. He continued on until soon he came to a clearing and in the distance a covered bridge. The area was famous for them, but he'd never found one so hidden, so deep. He studied it from afar as he kept walking toward it.

Covered in vines, the old bridge had seen better days. He focused on the plaque, now tarnished and hard to read overhead. 1920. He tipped his chin. This might be the oldest bridge he'd seen so far. He knew through his careful research that the oldest bridge, located in nearby Lincoln, was built in 1914 and was definitely on his list to see.

He ran his hand up and down the old wood trim as he admired the structure. Although it had seen better days, the romantic element of an era gone by left him breathless, shaken, and in awe. He walked around the side as far as he could, studying the sides. Chipped paint, dry rotted wood. He shook his head. "What a shame," he said. He took out his cell phone and snapped a few pictures before walking back. It was beginning to get darker, and he wanted to get back before he couldn't find his way.

~

Maggie tried to find something to do, but with his car still parked out there and getting dark soon, she worried about where he'd gone off to. She patrolled the small house. Finally, she grabbed her coat, tossed her scarf around her neck, and with her hands burrowed deep into her coat pockets, walked over to the park.

The small crossover bridge was the only way he would have been able to go deeper into the woods. She picked up her speed and hurried over the small bridge. It made her nervous every time she walked across it.

She made a mental note to ask the park service about repairing it.

She trudged up the small embankment, kicking leaves as she made her way down the very well-worn path. A small sign said the trail was approximately three miles to the bridge hidden by overgrown brush. She wondered if he even saw it.

She'd been on the trail numerous times, so she quickly walked it when she came face-to-face with Trey.

A startled look told her she'd taken him completely by surprise.

"Hey," she said, shaking off the chill of dusk.

"Hey. I just found the covered bridge. That's pretty exciting for something to be right in your backyard." They walked along the path side by side.

"Yes, I come out here often."

"So people do know about it?"

She laughed. "A few. I'm afraid with the sign covered in overgrown brush it's hard to know. The locals used to visit it a lot when I first moved out here. But now even they've stopped. The bridge is deteriorating badly with each passing day."

Trey lifted some of the peeling paint. "It's in pretty bad shape."

"The park doesn't have the money to refurbish every covered bridge. Most of the time it's private citizens or certain groups that raise funds to help renovate bridges."

They walked until they came to the narrow walkover, stopping before they crossed.

He motioned for her to cross over before him.

She trotted over and stood waiting.

"Well, it's a beautiful bridge. I can only imagine what it saw during its heyday." His eyes twinkled and made her heart flutter.

"You have a talent." She lowered her gaze and kicked a small gathering of leaves.

"Thank you. I just dabble. It helps me."

"I'm retired, so I'm trying to fill my days being productive instead of sitting on the couch eating cookies and watching Hallmark movies."

"Your camera," he said, raising his brows.

She hung her head. "They say a busy mind helps pass the time."

"I have my job to help keep me focused, but I'm still lonely too." He walked on ahead of her. He gathered his paints and put them away in the case, carefully taking down his painting. He touched a small edge to see if it was dry. He carried it and the small easel over to his parked car and began to put his things away. She leaned over and picked up the case and followed him.

"Yes, when I was working for the insurance

company it helped to fill my days. That and raising Collette, my daughter. But now I have so many hours to fill." She stepped away from the car.

He slammed the trunk down and rubbed his hands together. "Maybe you need a part-time job?" He dug his hands in his pockets and rocked on his heels. "It's getting cold out here."

"I don't want to be obligated to a job. Done that. Have the T-shirt." She bobbed her head and laughed at the very outdated joke.

"True. I guess with retirement comes freedom. Well, I better be going. It was nice meeting you. I hope the bridge gets some much-needed attention. So many of them do find backers and bring them back to their glory days."

"Maybe I'll look into that. That would definitely keep me busy." She shrugged.

"Good luck, Maggie Regan." He stepped to the driver's side and placed his hand on the car door.

"Bye, Trey Simmons. If you are ever back this way…" She flashed him a grin.

"For sure. I'll stop by, and we can have tea."

Maggie drew in a deep breath and held it. She stumbled on her words. "Would you like a cup of tea for the road?"

He withdrew his hand and twirled around.

She swore her heart stopped beating for a second. He dazzled her, made her head spin, and she wasn't sure if she was even breathing. A small gasp escaped her lips. *Breathe. Breathe, Maggie.* "It's cold, and I'd love the company."

He followed her into her house. She tossed another log onto the fire and stoked it. When flames began to shoot out from the logs, she crossed over to the kitchen. She sensed he might be looking at her. Normally it would cause her to feel insecure, but not this time.

She put the kettle on the stove and prepared the cups. He sat at the table and watched.

"I don't normally ask strange men to have tea with me." She didn't waver.

"Strange? I've been called many things, but strange isn't one of them," he teased, putting her at ease.

"Haha. Well played, Trey."

They sat at the table, holding their hot mugs of tea and talked about everything from the painting, the covered bridge, to his living conditions in San Francisco. It was a lively conversation, and Maggie was thoroughly entertained by all his crazy stories about city life. She had nothing to compare it to now that she lived in the outskirts of Eugene.

He shook his head. "I see all sorts of characters in the city. Down by the wharf, there is a guy who has spray painted his outfit silver and stands like a monument for spare change. There are musicians…who can't sing, or play an instrument, but still have their hand out, and of course there are the regular homeless people who are sleeping on cardboard boxes with tin cups for their change," Trey said.

Maggie frowned. "Wow. And right where the tourists are?"

"Unfortunately, yes. It's gotten bad the last couple of years. I don't like even going down there."

"Have you thought about moving out of the city—like to a smaller town?" She sank into the palms of her hands, resting her elbows on the table, her eyebrows lifting in harmony.

"I hate the traffic too. I'm walking distance from my office. So, I think I'll just have to suck it up. Well, I better be heading back. Thank you again for your hospitality, Maggie." He stood and began to walk slowly toward the front door.

"Anytime. I enjoyed our visit." She walked him out and stood on the porch.

"I did too." His gaze moved to her mouth and made her quiver.

"Seriously. Anytime," she found herself saying in a low, gravelly tone she didn't recognize. She swallowed quickly. "I mean, I'd like you to come visit again. I enjoyed it."

A warm smile traversed his face as he raised his palm and dashed a wave to her. She took a few steps and meandered toward the end of the porch, looking around the corner, watching him as he got inside his car. When he passed her by, she waved. With her head hung low, she walked back inside. She lowered herself onto the sofa, draping the afghan over her and watched the flames dance the night away.

CHAPTER 3

He gazed briefly in the rearview mirror. He wondered if she knew how beautiful she was. The way her eyes twinkled when she got excited, or the small giggle that made his heart ping. The way she played with her hands or the softness of her mouth. He tried to shake off the feelings, but something about Maggie Regan had him mystified and yearning for more. He drove a little faster, hoping it would get the images and feelings removed quicker but all it did was intensify this odd feeling he had for her.

Once back at the hotel, he devoured the sandwich and chips he purchased at the nearby shop while flipping through channels.

He showered and put on fresh jeans and a green T-shirt that showed off his physique. He worked out in the gym every day, and even while at hotels he sought out the exercise room. It was part of his therapy. Painting, exercise, healthy lifestyle, and unfortunately, some medication. His hope for the future was to ditch those meds, but right now they helped him sleep and keep the nightmares to a minimum.

He studied the covered bridge map the hotel clerk gave him. He wanted to see the oldest bridge before heading back to the city. He jumped in the car, set his navigation to the address, and set off for a day of exploring.

After driving for about two hours, he came across the famous bridge built in 1914, now located on private property thanks to a very dedicated and determined couple. They moved the bridge from its original location board by board to their Rose Lodge property, and with years of fund-raisers and a host of volunteers, the barn-red structure now served as a reminder of an era gone by and was visited by thousands each year.

He snapped several photos with his cell phone. As he took the pictures, a thought raced into his mind. The old bridge he came across deep in the woods near Maggie's. He wondered if anyone would be interested in restoring it. He knew it would only be a matter of time and that old bridge would be nothing but rubble. The dry rot was already very obvious.

He finished up taking pictures, took a quick glance around the small gift store, purchased a couple of post-cards and a glossy book about the origins of bridges around the country, and headed back to Eugene.

It was as if his car was on autopilot; it drove right to her house. He gripped the steering wheel and rested his head back. *What am I doing here?*

~

She'd been sitting on her front porch with a blanket across her lap, enjoying the outdoors when she saw him drive by. He headed down the road toward the parking area to the park. She stood, and stretching her neck as far as she could see, she watched his car come to a halt. She studied the car for movement but saw none. She shielded her eyes to see more clearly. Finally, after a few moments, he emerged from the car. She put her cup of tea down on the porch railing and watched as he moseyed toward her. His hips swayed gently, his strong glide coming closer, making her giddy with happiness. When he got in shouting distance, she waved and said his name loudly.

"Hello, Trey!"

He stepped into the yard, then ascended the few stairs to her porch.

"I hope you don't mind that I just dropped in."

Her face flushed hot. "Not at all. I told you, you were welcome anytime. Thought you were headed back to San Francisco. Tea?"

He followed her into the warm dwelling. She sensed he was staring again, but this time she felt much more relaxed and even a little bit sexy knowing he was looking.

~

He watched her move around the kitchen as she prepared their tea. He'd seen her go through the motions a few times now and never got tired of seeing her move. He gazed at her rounded hips, and he wondered if they were as soft as they appeared. He cleared his throat.

"I had one more stop to make before heading home. I made it out to the oldest covered bridge today."

She whirled around. "You went out to Lincoln?" She raised her brows, then leaned back onto the cabinet and countertop.

He eyed her body as she rested up against the cabinet. Her long dark hair tied back into a ponytail, and the dark jeans and plaid shirt she had on gave her a youthful look. Age was just a number anyway, right? He brushed his hand along his chin and realized he didn't shave again today. He had quite a bit of stubble going on.

"Yes, saw the Drift Creek Bridge." He pulled out a postcard and laid it on the table.

She crossed over to the table and picked it up. "I haven't been up there in years. It is a pretty bridge. What those folks did for that bridge was beyond incredible." She put the card back down.

"That's for you. I got it for you," he whispered.

The tea kettle whistled, making her turn away.

She slid the hot cup over toward him, then took a seat. "So you came back out here just to tell me you visited Drift Creek?" She dragged the cup to her lips and blew.

He rested back into the chair, shifting his weight. "It gave me an idea about the old bridge in the woods."

"Are you thinking what I think you're thinking?"

With his elbows on the table, he said, "I know it's crazy, but what if we restored that old bridge?"

"For one, it would bring a whole lot more traffic in here than I get now. The only thing that keeps me a little sane is when that green metal bar comes down, closing off the road to the park."

He nodded. "I didn't think about that. Maybe we could move your house?" He winked.

Maggie snorted, then laughed a hearty laugh. "Sure, that would be easy to do." She sipped her tea.

"I thought you liked the company the park brought. Giggling kids, happy families," he said, trailing off.

"Teens looking for a place to make out..." she added.

He put his tea down. The stillness of the room left them speechless. Her bottom lip quivered. He backed his chair out the same time she did. He came around the table, and she stood. He took her hands in his, and feeling her shake, he gently squeezed them.

"Maggie," he said softly.

She nodded, then traced her finger along his thumb.

He released his hold and pushed back. "I should be going. I'm sorry...I shouldn't have." He made his way toward the front door.

Maggie stood for a moment, trying to catch her breath. She whirled around. "Trey."

Trey held his hand on the doorknob.

"Trey," she called out, her voice getting closer.

He released his grip on the knob and turned to face her. "I'm sorry. I don't know what came over me."

She stepped into his space. "Don't be. I'm not offended by your gesture."

"I don't normally make passes at women that I've just met." The corners of his mouth drew up.

She moved toward him. "I don't usually ask men in for tea." She tilted her head and raised her brows. She reached for his hands. "I sense you're a good person though, and you paint beautiful images..." She nodded.

"You don't know anything else about me, though."

She cupped his hands. "I don't know what else is going on, but if you're broken in some way, I'm broken too. Maybe we can help each other."

He held her hands firmly. "Broken? How?"

Not taking her eyes off him, she told him the whole story of how her husband died.

"Your husband was killed when the Towers came down?" His voice shrieked, making her step back.

"Yes. Like so many others, he died that day."

With slouched shoulders, he dropped his head.

Maggie lifted his chin with her finger. "Now it's your turn."

"I'd just graduated from law school. Just hired by this great law firm. Regan, Scott and Matthews. My name, Simmons was going to be added. My fiancé and I were planning our wedding. There was miscommunication between her and me. I thought I was to meet her at her office, and she thought she was to meet me at mine. I'd already left the building when it happened. She was in the elevator going up to see me when the planes hit." A tear rolled down his cheek.

"Trey. My husband was Richard Regan of Regan, Scott and Matthews."

CHAPTER 4

The two stood in silence as they processed what just took place. This was monumental in so many ways. Was it a mere coincidence that Trey and Maggie were brought together, or was there a higher power intervening?

"Your husband was Richard Regan?" By Trey's puzzled look, it was obvious Maggie not only surprised him with this news but perhaps even shocked him.

She tipped her head. "Yes. What a small world. He told me he'd just hired a new attorney, and I vaguely recall him telling me your name. Everything has been such a blur since that day. It was as if my brain was wiped clean of so many thoughts and memories."

"I know what you mean. That's why I paint. My

therapist thought maybe it would help trigger some good memories and deal with my loss."

"Is that why you moved to San Francisco?"

He chortled. "I wanted to get as far away from New York as I possibly could."

"My good friend Katherine talked me into moving to Oregon. Collette was just a teenager and having a very difficult time in school. It was the second hardest thing I've done." She wiped the tears away when she recalled Richard's memorial service.

Trey embraced her tightly. "Well, I guess we're two lost souls who've found one another. Stranger things have happened."

She leaned back into his arms. "I'm happy to have found you, Trey Simmons. I hope you'll come back and visit me."

He released his hold and stepped back. "For sure." He turned and opened the door.

She watched him descend the couple of stairs from the porch and march on to his car. She drew her hand up in a wave and whispered goodbye. "Come back to see me, Trey Simmons," she called out.

"I will." Then he got inside his car and drove away.

She slowly closed the front door and walked into the kitchen. She stared out the window to where she'd seen him sit and paint. Now all that was left were piles of fallen leaves.

She began to rinse out the cups when her phone rang. She dried her hands and answered it.

"Maggie Regan!"

"Hello, Katherine. How are you?" She held the phone to her ear and walked around the small house.

"I'm good. I just wanted to wish you a happy Thanksgiving."

"You already wished me that. The other day when you called." She giggled.

"I did? Well, you can't have too many wishes, I suppose." Katherine snorted.

"Just cut to the chase, Katherine. You want to know if I have seen Trey."

"Trey?" Katherine's voice spiked an octave or two.

With a tone a bit on the disconcerting side, Maggie said, "The handsome young man who's been painting at the park."

"*That* Trey," Katherine said, playing along.

"I've seen him. I was going to call you later. Do you believe in a higher power?"

"Sure, I do."

"What about fate?"

"Yep."

"Well, it just so happens that Trey Simmons worked for Richard at the law firm. He'd just been hired."

Katherine gasped. "What?"

"I vaguely recall his name."

"And apparently Regan didn't ring a bell with him either," Katherine added.

"Nope."

"Why wasn't he in the building that day? I mean I'm glad he wasn't…"

"He'd left the building to meet his fiancé for coffee. They got their wires crossed, and she thought she was to meet him there."

"No!" Katherine bellowed.

"Yes," Maggie whispered.

"So, you both have this connection. That *is* really weird. In a cool way," Katherine said.

"I guess. He lives in San Francisco and just drove out here as something to do. He'd always wanted to visit Oregon. What are the odds he'd pick my park to paint in?"

"Not good. But good for you, I'd say." Katherine laughed.

"We're just friends, Katherine. Nothing more."

Maggie didn't have the courage to tell her the truth.

That she'd found Trey so very appealing in every way—from his broad shoulders to his strong hands, to his alluring eyes, Trey Simmons drew her in like a deep breath.

"Friends for now or friends with benefits?" Katherine giggled.

"Katherine Whittaker. Behave."

~

Maggie brought her famous sweet potato casserole and pumpkin cheesecake over to Collette and Jeremy's for dinner. Nothing said holidays like turkey, dressing, and all the other delicious foods cooking —mouthwatering aromas drifting room to room that awakened the senses.

Jeremy was putting another log on the fire when she entered the room. Rubbing her hands, she stood near him.

"Why is it no matter how full you think you are, when you enter a home that has been preparing for Thanksgiving, your mouth waters and your tummy rumbles?" She laughed then touched Jeremy on the arm.

"I know. I've been resisting eating anything today

just so I can have room for everything. Especially your sweet potato casserole."

"How sweet of you to say that." She tipped her chin, then crossed over to the kitchen where little Sam was helping set the table.

He could barely see above the edge of the table. He moved around the table, placing napkins, forks, and spoons.

"Maybe you can help him with the knives," Collette whispered.

Taking her cue, she rummaged in the silverware drawer pulling out three knives.

"You're doing such a great job, Sam." Maggie rustled up his hair while leaning over and kissing his rosy red cheeks.

"Nana!" he said, pulling away.

Collette and Maggie laughed.

"I've been so busy with Sam's preschool and Thanksgiving I haven't had a chance to talk with you. How are you?" Collette stirred the mashed potatoes on the stovetop.

"I'm good." Maggie leaned up against the counter and handed Collette the pepper.

Collette tapped the spice into the mixture and handed Maggie the container.

"Good. What have you been doing to stay busy? I

know the last time we talked you said you were getting a bit bored."

Maggie sighed. "Yeah, I've read every book on my shelves, every e-book on my Kindle, and now I'm just walking around the empty house trying to decide what to do with my time."

"I'd suggest the library but seems you might be a bit burned out on reading."

"I need a break, but I'll never give it up. I bought a camera."

Collette put the spoon down on the spoon rest. "A camera?"

"Thought maybe I'd take up photography."

"I think that's a great idea, Mom." She reached for something in an overhead cabinet.

"But I can only take so many photos. I need something else to do."

"What about knitting or crochet?"

Maggie frowned. "That would keep me inside. I need to get out more, Collette." She raised her voice unknowingly.

"Just an idea, Mom. Don't get excited."

"The walls are caving in on me, Collette," she blurted.

Collette braced her hands on her mom's arms. "I get that. I'm trying to be helpful. Don't bite my head off."

"I know you are. I'm just so alone. It's finally hit me. I'm going to die alone," Maggie said.

"No you're not. You have me, Jeremy, and Sam."

"You know what I mean, Collette."

Collette heaved her shoulders. "I think you should enroll in a dating service."

"A dating service?" Maggie placed her hands on her hips. "What makes you think that would work? Katherine tried to fix me up a couple times, and they were major disasters."

"Mom, finding your soul mate doesn't happen after the first date."

Maggie dropped her hands. That's what *she* thought. If only Collette knew how Trey seemed to fit the bill as a soul mate. She shook off the urge to tell her.

"I'll think about it."

"Jeremy, can you carve the turkey, please. Dinner is ready," Collette called out over her shoulder as she scooped the fully mashed potatoes into a serving bowl.

Dinner was lovely, and Maggie couldn't have chosen a better place to be during the holidays. Holidays were just another day until Collette and family came along. During dinner they chatted about the biggie, Christmas.

"Katherine is having a small Christmas party. She would like us all to come," Maggie said.

Collette's gaze traveled to Jeremy. Maggie watched as this spectacle between them played out. Jeremey nodded side to side, a mumbled grunt escaping his lips. "Children allowed?"

"I think so. She didn't say they couldn't. I'll double-check."

After dinner, Maggie helped Collette in the kitchen while Jeremy entertained little Sam. When the kitchen was neat and tidy, Maggie announced she should be going. It was getting late. Already well into dark, and she hated driving at night.

"Thanks for a lovely evening." She reached over the couch back and dropped a kiss on Sam's head, then she patted Jeremy's shoulder.

"Good night, Maggie," Jeremey said.

"Night, Nana!" Sam bellowed.

Collette walked Maggie to the door. "Call us when you get home. That road you live on is so dark."

"You used to live on that road once upon a time." Maggie's eyes sparkled.

"Yes, Mom, I remember." She leaned in and kissed her cheek.

Maggie gave her a backhanded wave while walking to her car.

*T*hanksgiving was just another day for Trey. He traipsed downtown after eating a cold turkey sandwich on dark rye. Besides the homeless people, Trey was the only one out. People were still enjoying oven-prepared turkey dinners, homemade apple and pumpkin pies, or sitting around the room playing cards or a board game while digesting their heavy but oh-so-joyful meal. He raised his collar around his neck, dipping his hands deeper into his pockets, breathing in the cool bay area air as he drifted along the battery like so many of the homeless people.

He'd done his best to avoid his mother's phone calls and gleeful voice of wishing him a happy Thanksgiving. Bah humbug. Wait. That's another holiday. He kept walking. He gazed toward the water. The sky held a chill with just a layer of fog still hanging around. He walked across the street. Shielding his eyes from the glare, he peered into some of the windows of the storefronts. On Black Friday the streets would be busy with holiday shoppers. He rather enjoyed this calm and quiet day. He walked up the main street that would take him to his apartment. There was a price to pay for living so close to the wharf, but he didn't care. It was only money. The best thing and the best years of his life were already taken. What's spending money on high-priced real estate going to do that losing your love hasn't? He picked up the pace and soon was home.

He tossed his jacket on the coatrack and entered the small and very modern apartment. With large windows to see out toward the bay and the city, a black leather sofa, glass and metal tables, and the color gray on walls and on the floor, Trey's apartment eluded to anything but cozy. More like cool and distant. He didn't spend a lot of time inside anyway. He found it hard to breathe when the walls began to cave in.

He worked four days a week at a law firm walking distance from his apartment. He only drove his car when he wanted to get out of the city. He walked every-where or took public transportation. He liked to mingle around people; he just didn't like to get too close to any one person. After he'd worked at the law firm for five years, people finally realized he was just a loner and left him alone. He was fine with that. No, he wasn't really. He'd get angry at himself when he would turn down invitations for dinner and other social events. But he never felt ready to just be the jovial guy he used to be. That day forever changed him.

He sat on his sofa and told his electronic compan-ion, Alexa, to play some jazz music. He picked up a book he'd been reading and immersed himself in the author's writing. His phone that sat on the glass coffee table lit up. He closed the book and answered the phone.

"Hi, Mom."

"I've been trying to call you. What's up?" Her voice was filled with concern.

"I went for a walk. I guess the cell service sucks out on the wharf," he said, telling her a little lie.

"Well, what did you do for Thanksgiving? Did you go over to any of your coworkers for a nice home-cooked meal?"

Trey leaned his head back. "No, I didn't go over to any of my coworkers' houses. You know I didn't. Why are you asking me that?"

"I guess because I hoped for once you'd change your mind and instead of wallowing in sadness, you'd surround yourself with smiling faces and good humor." She tried to hold back her stern tone, but it came floating through.

Trey sat forward. "Mom. I know you are worried about me…"

"You're damn right I am. You won't come home for the holidays, you won't invite us out there. I mean, Trey…what do you expect me to think? We're so far away, and we're worried." She was unsuccessful in holding back tears and began to sob.

"I'm sorry, Mom. I don't mean to upset you." Now

he felt like a total jerk for making his mom cry, but more importantly, for cursing. She rarely said swear words. "I tell you what. I'll come home for Christmas." There, he said it.

She sniffled into the phone. "You will?"

"Yes, I will."

They ended the conversation hospitably. She was happy he was coming home for Christmas, and he was happy to get back to reading his book.

~

When he walked into the law firm, the secretaries were already decorating for Christmas. Trey nodded to the women as they hung garland and lights, and another team was putting together a small artificial tree.

"Good morning, Trey," the pretty blonde who'd relentlessly flirted with him for months with no reciprocation on his part, called out.

He haphazardly waved to her then walked on to his small office. He opened up his laptop, took out a few papers from his leather briefcase and began to listen to his voicemail when the senior partner poked his head in.

Trey got a glimpse of the shadow entering the room.

While holding the phone to his ear, he mouthed good morning.

"I'll come back," Todd whispered.

Trey jotted down all the return calls he had to make, then went through his email. After he finished all that, it was lunchtime. He found Todd sitting in the break room talking with one of the other partners, Sean.

"Hey, Trey. Did you have a nice Thanksgiving?" Todd asked.

"I didn't do a whole lot. I just came back from a week in Eugene." He moved to the coffee pot on the counter and poured a cup.

"That's right. How was Eugene?" Sean asked.

Trey slid out a chair and sat. "It was fantastic. So green and beautiful. I scouted out some covered bridges and did a lot of painting."

"Great. Well, things are about to get slow around here with Christmas and all. Any plans?"

"Yeah, I think I'll fly back to New York and visit the folks."

Sean scooted his chair out from the table and stood. "It's been a while since you went back, hasn't it?"

Trey slowly nodded. "About five years."

"It's time, dude." Sean lifted his chin, biding both Todd and Trey goodbye, exiting the break room.

"Listen, Trey, I don't like to get too involved in my

employee's lives. You know that whenever you need time off, I'm good with that. As long as one of us is available to take calls from your clients and that sort of thing, you always have my blessing to go do what you need to do."

Trey wasn't stupid. He knew exactly what he was getting at. If he ever felt like he was about to crack wide open like some egg on the edge of a frying pan, he wanted Trey to know he could take some time off. He shrugged. "I'm good. A few days here and there and I'm like a brand-new person." He pushed his chair back and leaned forward to grab his cup. "I'll probably be heading back to Eugene soon." He stood.

"Oh?"

Trey glanced over to Todd. Carrying his coffee, he walked toward the door. "I met this person. She's different than anyone I've ever met before. We're just friends, but we have this common connection, and ever since I left her, she's all I can think about."

The two exited the break room together. "Connection? How so?" Todd asked.

"I don't talk about that day often, but in a nutshell, her husband had just hired me at the law firm in one of the Towers. She didn't know me, and I didn't know her. In fact, I had put the senior partner's name out of my mind, so I never put the two together when she told me her name."

"Well, that and she also lived in Oregon, why would you?" Todd raised his brows.

"Exactly. But anyway, I promised her I'd come back and see her. So I was thinking that maybe I would drive out to see her a week before Christmas and just fly from Eugene to New York to see my folks."

"Sounds good, Trey. Anything for you, man." He clutched his arm and squeezed it.

"Thanks, Todd. I appreciate it."

CHAPTER 5

Maggie left the house to go play with her new toy. It was a perfect time to try her new camera. She caught a squirrel digging in the earth, looking for a nut he'd most likely hidden some time ago. His beautiful, fluffy tail swooshed back and forth. Further down the well-traveled path, she came across a pile of dead tree limbs that formed an unusual monument. She stood back and took a few pictures at various angles. A snap of a dry branch had her suddenly look up and around. Everything in the woods stood still except for a few leaves that drifted and swirled to the ground. She shook her head, then put her eye to the window of her camera.

As much as she loved to be out in the woods, something about the quietness gave her chills. She finished her hike, then headed back home.

As she took one last picture of the very full creek that babbled over rocks and fallen tree limbs, she caught a glimpse of a car parked in the lot adjacent to the park. A man sat in the driver's seat. She followed the car with her gaze as she made her way back toward her house. Living alone, she was always aware of her surroundings. She never liked guns, but after Collette moved out, she realized living out in the country alone warranted her to be prepared. So when Katherine asked her to join her in learning how to safely fire a gun, she accompanied her to the range. Learning to shoot led to a purchase of a small handgun she kept in her nightstand drawer. A lot of good it did her when she was outside in the open with only a camera as her weapon.

The squeaky door stopped her dead in her tracks. Thank goodness for rusty hinges. Her eyes lit up. There stood Trey cloaked in a heavy coat, a woolen hat, and gloves.

He held up his hand and waved.

"Hey, Trey! I didn't expect to see you so soon." She made her way over to him, smiling ear to ear.

"Well, here I am. Seems I can't get enough…of this view." His gaze stayed on her.

This feeling between them, like a magnet to a piece of metal, made her stomach pitch. "Brr. It's cold outside." Bunching up her shoulders, she shivered.

"So I see you have your camera?" He rubbed his arms to keep warm.

Maggie fingered the camera she held. "Yes, I'm just fooling around, but I caught a few good images. Would you like to come in for a cup of tea or coffee?"

"I thought you'd never ask." He slid his arm around her as they walked toward her house.

Her willingness to fall into his embrace took her by surprise. She lowered her gaze and studied their feet as they hit the ground in unison, marching along kicking leaves as they breathed in the crisp air. When they got to the porch, they'd gone from embracing to holding hands. Trying to ward off the giddy feeling that transformed her from a middle-aged woman to something she'd not felt in a long time, she tempted him to follow with a hint of mischievousness.

She waltzed into the kitchen as she took off layers of warm clothing, draping them over the back of the couch and on the back of the kitchen chair. She immediately took the kettle off the burner and began filling it.

"Do you mind putting a couple of logs on the fire?" Her voice, filled with joy, echoed in the small room.

"Not at all," he yelled out as he scrutinized every corner in search of wood.

"Outside," she shouted. "I have it stacked on the side of the house."

Trey went in search of wood, leaving her to get the tea ready.

She dunked the cinnamon and orange teabags in the hot water. She drew in the warming scent.

In a few minutes, he came in with an armful of logs. He let them roll off his thick arms, and Maggie couldn't keep her eyes off his solid frame. He tossed a log on the fire, then joined her in the kitchen. "Something smells good," he said, picking up one of the mugs.

"Cinnamon and orange." She blew the hot liquid. "So, you're going to go see your parents. That's good. I'm sure they'll enjoy that." She tapped the table, letting him know to sit.

He slid out a chair and joined her. "Yeah, she guilted me into coming."

"Your mom?" Maggie tossed her head back and laughed.

Trey nodded slowly as he sipped the hot beverage.

"Cookies. I almost forgot." She slid her chair out abruptly and went to the pantry. "Oatmeal or chocolate chip?"

"Oatmeal," he said. "Maggie, I haven't stopped thinking about you since my last visit."

She held her breath as she contemplated her answer. She exhaled softly. "I've thought about you a lot too." She joined Trey at the table with the cookies.

"I know it's crazy. I mean we just met and all, but I feel drawn to you in a way I can't explain."

"Do you think it's because of Richard?"

"I don't know. Maybe, but I think it's more than that." His eyes darkened, making her feel weak.

She cupped her hand to stop the trembling. "I've been alone for a very long time."

"I have too."

"Whatever we do, we need to take it slow. I can't risk…"

"Risk what? Feeling alive again after feeling so alone? I, for one, welcome it. I'm tired of always feeling like I'm one step away from the last day of my life. I want to be happy again, see everything in a positive light, love again."

Her breath hitched as she moved away from his smoldering eyes.

"Maggie, am I scaring you by wearing my feelings on my sleeve?"

She drew her gaze back to his and this time she reached across the table and opened her hands.

He laced his fingers with hers, drawing make-believe circles on the base of her thumb. "You're trembling, Maggie."

"I haven't felt this strong of an attraction in a long time. I don't know what to do with it." She withdrew her fingers from his embrace, crossing her arms at her chest, hugging them snug.

He slid back his chair, releasing his hands and moved around the corner of the table. He lifted her up by the arms and pulled her in close. The temptation to flee was so strong she stepped back. She glanced nervously at him under her lashes. She took a few slow breaths, calming her racing pulse and fluttering stomach.

Stepping into her circle, he reached up and stroked her hair. "I won't hurt you, Maggie. I promise." His low and gravelly tone made her tongue-tied. She stumbled, searching for the words.

"I'm just…"

He devoured her mouth with a deep and sensual kiss, stopping her from finishing her sentence. Parting her lips, she let him in, slipping her hands behind his head, holding him there as they kissed. Suddenly she dropped her hands and stood back, clearing her head of the cobwebs and steadying her breathing.

She quickly turned away, her fingertips resting on her swollen lips.

"Maggie," he said, touching her back.

She rubbed her arms absently, then crossed them.

"Maggie," he said again, turning her toward him.

Looking up and meeting his gaze, she dropped her arms and leaned in, finding his mouth. She kissed him with all the passion she held.

CHAPTER 6

They cuddled on the sofa, watching the flames, darting back and forth in the fireplace. Soft music played in the background. If not satisfied by the tea and cookies, the air of contentment swirling around them after surrendering to deeper feelings, Trey and Maggie drifted off into a magical place that both of them needed.

The crackling of wood comforted her as she snuggled in his arms. "I've been thinking about that bridge." Her tone was pillowy and hung in the warm air.

Trey picked up his legs and set them on the table, crossing them at the ankle.

"Maybe the park service would allow volunteers to spruce it up."

"Hmm."

She leaned forward and turned toward his profile. "You know. Get a group of dedicated people together, raise money, and little by little restore the bridge." She blinked a couple of times.

Trey didn't move a muscle, his gaze glued to the roaring fire. "What about all the people coming to see it."

"That's the price I'm willing to pay to see it through. That bridge is too important to just let rot."

His hands carved through his hair, holding it back, releasing it and releasing a grumble of sorts. "Let's think it over. I admit I was all over it after visiting Drift Creek. But you're right. It's a pretty big undertaking." He ran his hand along the outer side of her thigh.

She placed a finger under his chin and turned him toward her. He reached over and pushed away hair that had fallen down almost into her eyes. "You're so beautiful any time of the day, but in this fire-lit room, you're even more beautiful." He leaned forward and kissed her. He started to move away but in a quick movement, she stopped him by holding his head in place, and soon the discussion of bridges was just a fleeting thought replaced with warm kisses full of desire.

She stood at the door and waved goodbye to Trey. But this time she knew he'd be back. She reached up and touched her lips. She closed the door and moved her back up against it, plonking her head back onto the hard surface of the door. The ring of her phone startled her. She skipped softly to the other room to retrieve her phone.

"Maggie Regan, I'm so happy for you!" Katherine said.

"I guess the attraction was real."

"Of course it was real. Do you think he'd have come back just for tea and cookies?" She laughed. "I mean if they were homemade, maybe, but you buy those sugary store-bought kind."

"Katherine! But yes, I do believe he's sincere. What do I tell Collette?"

"Collette? You don't tell her a thing right now. It's too new. I mean what if something...I mean..." She tried to soften her anxiety. "Just wait a while. You don't owe Collette any explanation."

"True, I don't, but she's my daughter, and just during Thanksgiving she suggested I enroll in a dating service. So

I think she'd be okay with me dating Trey. Even though he's younger. A lot younger," she added, the tone of anguish prevalent in her realization of their age difference.

"Age is just a number, Maggie. You two were drawn together. Be it fate, a higher power, whatever. This is just too real to ignore. I'm happy for you. So is he coming back?"

"Yes, he's staying at the hotel at the edge of the parkway near town. He's flying to New York in a couple of days."

"So this is a stopover on the way to New York?"

Maggie knitted her brows. Something about the way her friend said that cheapened their feelings. "Katherine, it's not like that."

"I didn't mean anything by it, darling. This is two thousand and eighteen, no worries. Call it whatever you all want. I say get it while you can."

"Katherine Whittaker. I am at a loss for words right now."

Katherine laughed into the phone. "You can take the girl out of the city, but you can't find a big enough piece of tape to cover her mouth!" She hooted into the phone again, making Maggie grin.

How did opposites ever get together, Maggie wondered. She was quiet, enjoyed candlelit dinners, warm fires blazing in the background, soft music piped in from a distance, the sounds of night as they crept into her windows, and the feel of cool water from the babbling creek during the heat of summer. Katherine enjoyed loud music, crowds of people, and if she dipped her feet in anything, it would be a bathtub full of bubbles surrounded by candles and a bottle of the best champagne money could buy.

"It was nice talking to you, Katherine. I'll let you go. We'll talk again soon." She smacked a kiss into the receiver, then ended the conversation.

"You're coming over for the little get together, right?"

She'd almost forgotten. "Yes, we'll be there."

Who was he kidding? Sleep was the last thing on Trey Simmons' mind. He continuously played the part over and over in his mind when he jumped up from the table and devoured her mouth. Well, it didn't exactly happen that way, now did it? He played it again. He slowly made his way over to her and took her trembling body into his embrace. He lovingly slid back the drooping hair that fell into her eyes, and when they locked gazes, he leaned forward and kissed her.

He tossed and turned thinking about her nonstop. What was he going to do? He lived in San Francisco, and she lived here in Eugene. Everyone knew long-distance relationships rarely survived. He sat up in the bed, fluffing up his pillow behind him. He stared at the bedside clock. He wondered if she was awake. It was only a little after eleven. He picked up his cell phone and called her.

"Hello?"

"Hi, Maggie. I hope I didn't wake you."

"Trey?"

"I couldn't sleep. I…I just needed to hear your voice one more time."

"That's okay. I was having a difficult time falling asleep as well. I'm glad you called."

"We have one more day together before I fly to New York. Why don't I pick you up and we can explore some trails. Bring your camera."

"I'll pack a lunch for us too."

"Maggie?"

"Uh-huh?"

He sensed her half-asleep tone, so he quickly finished the conversation. "I'm happy we met."

"I am too. See you tomorrow. Good night."

CHAPTER 7

She packed a lunch that consisted of bologna and cheese sandwiches, a can of Pringles, and a baggie of Fig Newton's. She tossed in a handful of paper napkins and small paper plates. She strummed her finger along her jawline. Then she crossed over to the cabinet that held the bottle of wine she'd had for a while. She searched her junk drawer and pulled out the corkscrew and went on the hunt for some plastic glasses. She lifted the bag and zipped it shut, then carried it to the living room.

The weather report said it would be extremely cold with a chance of snow flurries. She dressed in layers and waited for Trey.

A couple of times an unfamiliar noise had her rushing to the window, hoping it was him. Peering in between the blinds, she searched the area. No Trey. She let the blinds drop into place, then moved away.

She'd just moved away when a honking sound giving her reason to rush back to the blinds and take a peek. She moved away from the window, grabbed the large thermal bag packed with their lunch and her camera, and crossed over to the front door. When she opened it wide, there he stood dressed in thick outer garments with his beanie cap almost covering his eyes. A white puff of air circled his mouth when he spoke.

"It's cold today," he said, shivering.

"You Californians aren't used to this cold weather, are you?" She laced her arm in his.

"Not like this."

They walked to his car where he helped her get in. Then they took off for a day of exploring.

"You've lived here for a long time. Where should we head to?"

Being this close to him spun up raw feelings. She brushed the goose bumps away.

She directed him to a place she'd been to a couple of times, the Delta Ponds Park. It was a perfect place for birdwatchers with all the ponds, channels, and wetlands. Maggie hoped the cold weather would keep all the humans away and they could enjoy the quietness of the area. Bordering on a stretch of the Willamette

River, it was home to many birds and other wildlife, making it a great place to take pictures.

Christmas carols played on the radio as they traveled. They made small talk, but it was hard to find something to start a conversation with. Right now, the attraction she had for him was raw and unfounded. They needed something to grow this relationship if it were to go anywhere. It couldn't just be a sexual attraction. That would be...awful? She rolled her head toward the window, hiding her immoral grin.

She was the same kind person, but she saw things differently after 9-11. Life was too short, and she was tired of being alone.

"Turn here," she said, snapping out of her dream state.

Trey did a 90-degree turn into a driveway that led up a steep hill, finally leveling off to a paved parking lot. Two other cars were also parked. Maggie frowned.

"What's wrong?" Trey asked as he unbuckled his seat belt.

"I was hoping we'd be alone. But I guess you can't keep the avid birdwatchers away." She giggled.

She stayed focused on Trey as he rummaged around in his trunk. She ogled his broad shoulders, her gaze drifting to the back of his head where his thick hair curled up at the ends just above his collar. She looped the camera strap over her head.

"I never go home without these. You never know when you'll see something worth painting." He lugged the easel out and sat it down, going back inside the trunk and retrieving a black box with a handle.

"You have to have a lot of patience for what you do," Maggie said.

They began to explore the area by crossing over a bridge, then walking down a pathway that led them to the first pond. Two men sat on canvas stools with binoculars.

"Good afternoon," Maggie said as they walked by.

The grunted and nodded, then turned back to bird-watching.

They found a quiet spot where Trey set up his easel. She snapped pictures of birds and a turtle that floated around on a limb, trying to find one ray of sun amid the mostly gray sky to warm his body. She focused on a tree that had a beautiful shape to its trunk that if you looked at it hard enough, it took on an appearance of a face complete with features.

She leaned over Trey's shoulder and watched him as he drew the paintbrush up down and all around the canvas. It was a beautiful sight to see him when he worked. He'd occasionally look up above his canvas, then his gaze would drop back down. He was painting a picture of the pond. The way he blended the blues for the pond and the browns for the tree trunks left her in awe.

"You have a talent, Trey," she said, resting her hands on his shoulder.

He reached up and cupped her hands, holding them in place. The tingling sensation his touch brought to her was surreal but very welcomed.

"Let me know when you're hungry." She pulled her hand out from his.

He nodded, then went back to work, leaving her with her thoughts and fantasizing about him and what this thing they were doing was.

She moseyed down the path to find more picture-perfect moments. Startling her, a squirrel ran past her and up a tree nearby. She quickly got into action with her camera and clicked away. She moved further down the path where she discovered a small flowering plant shielded by a large rock, holding on to dear life after the freezing temperatures. She snapped a photo of the lavender beauty against the gray stone, marveling at the wonders of Mother Nature.

"Maggie!"

She turned when she heard her name shouted.

"Yes, I'm here." She moved fast toward his voice.

"I was worried about you. You wandered off." Trey held her by both arms.

"I didn't go far. I just got carried away taking pictures is all." Her eyes fluttered as she rested a hand on his wrist. "I'm not going anywhere, Trey."

He tipped his chin. "How about that lunch now?"

They feasted on the lunch she'd literally thrown together. It wasn't what you'd call a fancy lunch by any means, but he seemed to enjoy the bologna sandwich and her obsession with Pringles. They sipped the wine she'd added at the last minute from red plastic cups so no one would be the wiser. It seemed to do the trick and warm them up from the inside out.

After they finished eating, Trey asked her for a very personal favor. At first, she said no, but when he seemed hurt by her refusal, she gave in.

After she'd sat there for almost an hour, trying to be supportive of both his creativity yet stay warm in the very cold temperatures, she broke the silence.

"I'm cold, Trey. How about we finish this another time."

"I'm almost finished," he said.

She watched him with his tongue gripped between his teeth and his chest rising and falling with each meticulous stroke of his brush.

He stepped back and admired his work, then waved her over to see it.

Her jaw slowly dropped as she eyed the painting. She turned her gaze up to him. "You did that in just an hour?" She laced her arm with his.

"When you have a beautiful subject such as your-self, you have to paint fast."

Sliding her free hand behind his neck, she drew him in for a kiss. The cool touch of his lips roused her senses. He pressed his body closer, closing the gap between them, teasing her with sensual kisses and making her fully aware of his desire for her. Red leaves swirled down around them, and the chilly breeze pushed them closer and closer, while in the distance songbirds serenaded them.

~

Maggie stood back and watched as he put his things away. She followed his every movement, and when he caught her lovingly star-ing, he winked at her. Her hand covered her warm cheeks, trying to hide her obvious blushing. He made her feel so young and carefree.

They walked hand in hand back to his car. When he leaned into the trunk to put the easel away, she couldn't resist studying him from the back. Lean but strong with deliberate movements. She rubbed at a tic above her left eyebrow when he caught her staring. *That was close!*

The ride back to her house became awkward when a string of holiday songs came on the radio that reminded her of a different time. Her memories of Christmas in New York. The time they went to Times Square or took in a Broadway show. She turned away, hiding the tears. Why couldn't she get past this feeling of sorrow? It'd been seventeen years. Maybe she didn't want to move forward? Maybe she was sabotaging her own chance at happiness!

"Well, here we are." He cut off the engine and turned his body slightly.

Maggie unbuckled her belt and turned, leaning her back up against the car door.

"Are you going to invite me in?" He rested his hand on her leg.

"I'm not feeling that great at the moment. I'm sorry, Trey. Maybe another time." She turned to open the door, but he stopped her with his hand on her arm.

"Maggie, what's wrong? Did I say something to offend you?"

She shook her head.

"Then what? Everything was great up at the Delta

Pond Park. I don't understand. First you want me, then you push me away."

"I know, I'm sorry. I'm confused."

"You didn't seem too confused when you kissed me." His stern voice made her cry softly.

She brushed away the tears and opened the door. "I know. I didn't mean to be a tease. I do like you. I mean this has been great. It's what I've been praying for. To find someone to make me feel whole again. But then…"

"But then what?" he whispered.

"All the memories come crashing through. I don't know. Am I allowed to be happy again?"

"Of course you are, Maggie. Richard would want you to be. I know Lacy would want me to be. I admit it's taken me a long time to realize that. I felt guilty for what happened. But I didn't crash a plane into that building. The only thing I did was…"

She closed the door and faced him. "The only thing you did was love her."

Running his hand through his hair, he pushed his head back into the seat rest and grunted. Tears bobbled under his bottom lid. Finally, a stray one trickled down his cheek. He quickly brushed it away.

"Trey. Neither one of us asked for this tragedy, but both of us are living with the aftermath. I loved Richard. With all of my heart. Sure, we had our ups and downs, but he was my rock. And when Collette and I lost him, we lost a part of us too."

"I know. I guess the same can be said for me and Lacy. Although we hadn't started our life together, she was the one. I knew it, and I couldn't wait for her to be my wife."

"So, where do we go from here?" She arched her brows.

"I'm getting on a plane and going to New York. I have some unfinished business there. When I come back, we'll talk."

She lowered her gaze.

He lifted her chin with his finger. "We'll get the kinks all worked out, I promise." He leaned in and kissed her.

~

Turned out the holiday party Katherine was giving was totally family friendly. She even got her husband to dress up like the jolly old man himself. Sam was super happy to sit on Santa's lap. When Santa did a quick change and came out as Katherine's husband, Sam was too smart for that. He eyed him up and down, finally recognizing his wedding band as the same one Santa had on, and blew his cover!

Everyone fell out laughing. Maggie bent over gasping from laughter and grabbed her side. "Stop. That's so funny. It's just what I needed tonight too."

"That and this eggnog," Katherine said, toasting Maggie.

"Yeah, it's pretty tasty too."

"Okay. Now that I've gotten you in a corner, what about the mystery guy?"

Maggie blushed. It could have been from the eggnog, but it probably was about the dumb feelings she created for this guy. "Good." She took a sip of the creamy drink, wiping the whipped cream from her lip with her tongue. "This is yummy."

"Just good. That's all I'm going to get is good?" Katherine frowned.

"I'm falling for him," she said, whispering into Katherine's ear.

"I knew it." Katherine wrapped her arm around Maggie's shoulders.

"It's probably the dumbest thing I've ever done. I mean who goes out of their way to speak to a guy in a park?"

"Not just any guy, Maggie. A hottie from what you tell me. He lured you. That's what hot guys do. I'm just jealous."

Maggie cut her friend a sharp look. "Katherine, this

is not about his hotness." Who was she lying to? Herself or Katherine? She shook her head wildly. "Well, maybe it is. Just a little." She let out a husky laugh.

"It's not dumb, Maggie. It's fate. I'm a true believer in fate. And faith. You have to have a little bit of both." Katherine leaned in and kissed her cheek. "I have enough for both of us, so I'll just wave my magic wand." She played like she was putting some spell on Maggie, then laughed.

"No more eggnog for you," Maggie said, knitting her brows.

Maggie rummaged through all the boxes stacked in the garage, ones labeled Christmas. Covering her mouth, she stifled the sneeze from all the dust. She opened the flaps and lifted paper-wrapped items, carefully folding back layers. Her eyes lit up when she saw the snowmen she used to display. She set them aside, retrieving the next item. She moved to the next box, and with one giant blow, blew the dust off it before opening it. Inside, she found the nativity scene and boxes of ornaments.

She made a couple of trips inside with her newfound items and began to set them around the living room. She draped garland over the kitchen window and set a Christmas tree made from a large pine cone, that

Collette had made in elementary school, on the windowsill. While she decorated, she hummed along to the Christmas songs that played from the very old radio she had with a broken antenna, and when everything had a spot, she stepped back with her hot cup of tea and admired her now festive house. The only thing missing was a tree.

~

She walked up and down the paths scattered with pine leaves and string, looking for the right one. Parents with their children giggling as they searched for the perfect tree reminded her how children's laughter helped soothe the soul. She remembered those days clearly. She shook off the sneaking sadness that reared its head and continued the search for her tree.

"Can I help you, miss?" a friendly voice said.

Maggie jerked her head up to find a redheaded young man probably about twenty years old with freckles, wearing a red stocking hat that said Ho Ho on it. She couldn't help but laugh at the missing third Ho.

"Love your hat," she said. "I'm looking for about a five-foot tree. It has to be full, no dead branches." She reached in and tugged a tree out of the bunch. "This one looks good." She continued to twirl it around, but it began to sway, and the young man grabbed it.

"Here let me do that for you." He whirled it around so she could see all sides.

"Yes. That's perfect. I'll take it."

"Let me wrap some twine around it, and I'll carry it to your car."

"Is it heavy?" She tapped her finger to her chin, trying to figure out how she was going to get that tree inside her house.

"It's not heavy. Just kind of cumbersome."

She looked on while the tree attendant wrapped up her tree nice and tight. Maybe she'd ask Jeremy for help.

After the tree was secured to her rooftop, Maggie headed home. Once she pulled into her driveway, she began to untie the young man's knots and loosen them. She thought better of it when she realized she probably needed some help and decided to call Collette.

hile Jeremy got the tree down from her car roof, Maggie gave Collette and

Sam the ten-cent tour of her newly decorated house. Sam kept touching things and giggling.

"Mom, everything looks so festive. What made you decide to decorate?" She picked up one of the snowmen.

"I decided it was time. I've always enjoyed your home for the holidays. I always said I didn't have time to bother with decorations, but the truth was, I just didn't want to open the boxes of memories." She laced her arm around Collette's waist.

"Well, it looks lovely. You should invite Katherine over. She'll love what you did with the place."

Jeremey, breathing heavily, lugged the tree inside. "Where do you want it?" He peered in between branches, looking for guidance.

Both women at the same time pointed to the corner. "Over there, Jeremey," they said in unison, motioning to the tree stand.

Jeremy, with the help from the women, got the tree in the stand. Collette filled a pitcher of water and emptied it into the stand.

"Since you all are here, do you want to help me decorate the tree?"

Collette's gaze dropped to her watch.

Maggie glanced at hers. "It's dinnertime. Let me

think," she said, cocking her head. She hadn't thought much about eating lately. "I think I have a frozen pizza in the freezer."

So while Sam nibbled on pepperoni slices, Jeremy strung the lights and watched the women put the ornaments on. Every time one evoked a special memory, they talked about it while hanging it.

The two women huddled as they admired the final production of the decorated tree.

"It's pretty, Nana," Sam bellowed.

"It sure is, Sam!" Maggie replied. "And soon enough there will be presents under it for you."

~

The very next day, Maggie took off to the local mall. She purchased a few items that Collette said were on Sam's wish list. She found a pretty scarf for Collette and a pair of leather gloves for Jeremy. And even though she wouldn't see Trey until after Christmas, she purchased various sized canvases and some brushes the art store employee said were top of the line.

Satisfied with her shopping experience, Maggie headed home to wrap. *Wrapping paper!* She stopped at the dollar store near her house and picked out a couple of rolls, some tape, and ribbon. Sam would just tear his packages open, and she doubted he'd care where she purchased the paper at. For that matter, no one would care.

She rolled out the paper on the bed and cut the sheets to fit the items. One by one, she wrapped them. Piled high under her chin, she carried the packages to the living room and carefully placed them around the tree. "Now Christmas can come."

~

On Christmas Eve as she was about to put the lasagna in the oven, her phone rang. She thought it might be Collette telling her they were running late. She immediately recognized the number.

"Hey," she said in a steady and even tone.

"Hi. How are you?"

"I'm well, thank you. How's New York?"

"Good."

"Your folks?"

"Fine."

"What's wrong, Trey?"

"Nothing. Everything is just great now that I've heard your voice."

She exhaled the breath she'd been holding. "Your short answers concerned me."

"I wish you were here, or I was there. Something like that." He laughed.

"I know. Collette and family are coming over tonight. I'm making lasagna, and we're going to watch Sam open gifts. It's the first time I've had a real tree in seventeen years. I went all out and decorated for the holidays."

"That's a step in the right direction."

"I'll take a picture with my phone and send it to you." Maggie hunted around for her phone.

"No worries. I'll let you get back to getting dinner ready for your family. I just wanted to say hi. I miss you."

"I miss you too. Hurry back to me, okay, Trey?"

~

Every now and then her mind drifted to him. His strong arms holding her tight, and the way he trailed kisses up and down her neck. She shuddered thinking about his touch.

"You want me to put another log on the fire, Maggie?" Jeremy asked, breaking her fantasy.

"Please. That would be nice." She absently rubbed her arms, trying to stay warm and also focused.

After dinner, they opened gifts.

"Nana!" Sam said, opening up his Batman cape and quickly wrapping it around his shoulders as he ran through the house. All the adults laughed.

"There's another one that goes with that," she sang out, getting his attention back to the brightly colored gifts.

Sam retrieved one from deep under.

"That's for your daddy," Maggie said.

Sam trotted over and dropped the small box onto Jeremy's lap.

"Thank you, Maggie," he said, immediately trying the brown leather gloves on.

"You're very welcome."

Sam retrieved another one out from under the tree, huffing and puffing.

"Mommy," Maggie directed.

Maggie watched carefully as Collette unwrapped her gift.

"Mom. It's absolutely beautiful. I love it." She flung the scarf around her neck, pulling Maggie in for a hug.

"There's only one left," Sam announced.

"Must be for you, kiddo." Maggie sat back and crossed her arms. Her Cheshire grin made Sam giggle.

He tore open the paper and pulled out the Batman mask. His face lit up to a brilliant red as he studied it. "Thank you, Nana." He popped it on, then came over to her for a kiss. The group fell out laughing as he tried to kiss Nana through the mask.

"Sam, take the mask off," Jeremy said, laughing.

The evening took on a slower pace after the opening of gifts. Sam nestled in the crook of Jeremy's arm, with Jeremy keeping one eye open as the women talked. He'd occasionally grunt or give a one-word answer letting them know he was still awake, barely.

"Mom, thank you for everything. I know this wasn't easy for you." Her gaze drifted around the room.

"I wish I'd done it before now." Pausing between each word she added, "So many wasted years." She lowered her gaze and swallowed down the lump that formed in her throat. Trembling just a little, she told Collette in her most steady and calm voice about Trey.

After a long pause, Collette spoke. "Does your mystery man have a name?"

"Yes. Trey Simmons."

"Does he live here?"

"No. San Francisco."

Jeremy grumbled.

Maggie's gaze drifted toward him. "He's originally from New York." She intertwined her hands repeatedly, waiting for more grunts from Jeremy or squeals from Collette.

"What brought him to the Eugene area?" Collette crossed her legs and arms, her overly protective daughter mode kicking in now.

"He came out here for a little vacation and liked the area. Yes. It's rather strange how it all came to be. He was painting at the park across the street. You should see his paintings. He's really gifted." Her mind drifted to her portrait.

"When can we meet him?"

Maggie blinked, and her oval face flushed hotly. "Soon."

Collette gave Jeremy the sign to get up.

Jeremey picked up a sleeping Sam from the sofa and slung him over his shoulder. He never even opened his eyes until they were outside and the cold air hit him. His head popped up. "See you tomorrow, Nana, after Santa Claus comes," Sam yelled, then plopped it back down.

Maggie laughed. "See you tomorrow, Sam."

Collette leaned over and kissed her mother's cheek. "I love you, Mom. I want you to be happy."

"I am happy. Every day I'm happier than the last."

"I look forward to hearing more about Trey." She turned and walked away.

"See you tomorrow," Maggie shouted.

~

Maggie woke up feeling like the Energizer Bunny. Even though the air was crisp, she bundled up and took a walk. She grabbed her camera at the last moment just in case. She took her normal path to the bridge, but when she got to it, she noticed someone had spray-painted bad words all over the side of it. *Who'd do such a thing?*

She inspected the damage a bit further. Feeling a bit uneasy being in the woods alone, she glanced around. She didn't see anyone, and except for the sounds of leaves falling and the occasional broken twig, she was the only breathing thing nearby. She snapped some pictures of the graffiti and headed back to her house.

When she went over to Collette's and Jeremy's for dinner, she shared what she'd discovered. After a little convincing, Maggie reported it to the police. It was Christmas Day, so they promised to send an officer out the next day to take the report and look at the crime scene.

It was hard to outdo Christmas Eve at Nana's house, but Santa came through for Sam. So with all the new stuff he got, he had plenty to entertain him. Maggie helped Collette clean up the kitchen. Her hand flew to her mouth to hide a yawn telling them she wanted to get back home before it became dark.

"Call us when you get home, Mom. In light of what happened at the park, I want to know you got inside okay."

"Will do, hon. But you know I've lived out there for a long time. Never had an ounce of trouble before."

"These are different times, Maggie," Jeremy said.

Maggie walked down the hall toward Sam's bedroom where she found him playing with all his new toys. "Nana is headed home."

Sam jumped up and wrapped his arms around her neck. "I love you," he squealed.

"I love you too."

While Jeremy and Sam stayed inside, Collette walked her mother to her car.

"Thanks for a lovely evening." Maggie hugged her daughter.

"I wish you'd come over more often. You know you're always welcome." She gave her a *you have no excuse* look.

"I know. I appreciate that. Talk to you soon." She dropped a kiss on her cheek. "You better get back inside. It's cold." She got inside her car and dragged the seat belt over her lap, clicking it closed. She started the engine, adjusted the heat and as she drove away, she waved goodbye, feeling a tad blue she was going home to four walls and a lot of quiet.

~

She inserted the key in the door lock and wiggled it. Just then her cell phone went off. She grunted. "Collette. I told you I'd call when I got inside." She pushed open the door and then locked it behind her. With her back up against the door, she retrieved her phone from her purse. It wasn't Collette.

"Hey, Trey," she said, breathless.

"What's wrong? Why are you out of breath?"

"I was trying to get inside fast, and then the phone started ringing."

"Why were you trying to get inside fast?" Trey asked.

"It's cold outside." She began to take off her layers as she held the phone to her ear.

"Okay. I thought something happened."

"Something did. But I wasn't going to share it with you right now."

"Well now you must. I won't let you off the phone until you do." A wicked little laugh came through the line.

"Someone sprayed graffiti on the bridge."

"Really? Did you see anyone?"

"No, that's the strange part. Never heard a car or saw anyone."

"When I get back, I'm going to install a camera and lights on your house."

She paused. "When you get back here? When is that?" She knitted her brows.

"First things first. I'm calling you because I have a crazy idea. I hope you'll do it."

"I'm listening."

"Fly out and be with me for New Year's Eve."

She gasped then stuttered. "Trey…I don't…"

"Please." His sexy tone melted her heart and made her knees wobble.

"I don't have anything to wear."

"That won't be a problem." More of the sexy tone came through, this time melting every inch of her.

She held her breath as crazy thoughts whirled around in her head. What would she tell Collette? Her lonely mother is running off to New York to be with a much younger man. That might not go over too well.

"Trey, I don't know."

"I've never begged any woman before in my life. I'm begging you. Please come to New York."

She glanced around the room, the remnants of

Christmas Eve still fresh in her mind. She crossed into the kitchen. The angles of her mouth curved upward, the outer corners of her eyes crinkled as she observed the pine cone tree splashed with glitter sitting on her windowsill. She swallowed the lump down in her throat, and squaring her shoulders to help her feel brave, she squeaked out a yes.

"Yes, I'll come. Tell me where to meet you."

CHAPTER 9

She called Katherine and told her all about her upcoming trip to New York. Of course, she had a lot of suggestions as to what to say and do, none of which Maggie anticipated doing. She nodded and occasionally said a yes or a no as she walked around the room, holding the phone. She peered into her closet, strumming her hand through the hanging clothes, picturing possible outfits for her suitcase.

"I'm not purchasing a negligée. You're so…I don't know, crazy, I guess.

"Don't tell me that's not on your mind. It's been how long, Maggie?"

Maggie's cheeks burned. "It's not like that, Katherine."

"He's a man, isn't he? A younger man too."

Maggie frowned. "I need a new dress. Something that sparkles for New Year's Eve."

"Let's go shopping," Katherine said.

~

Katherine picked her up the next day. If Maggie didn't absolutely need the dress, she'd have avoided the mall like the plague. It was packed with shoppers returning unwanted Christmas gifts.

"I must have been out of my mind agreeing to this," Maggie said as she made her way in and around a sea of frustrated shoppers.

"It'll be worth it when you find the most beautiful dress," Katherine said, looking through racks of clothes. "What about this one?" She held out a leopard print dress with a low neckline.

Maggie shot her an angry look.

"Maggie. Live a little."

Maggie paused, lifting her gaze from a rack of dresses. She wrinkled her brows. Live a little. What the heck did she think she was doing now. She began her search again for the perfect dress.

Armed with six dresses, Maggie made her way toward the dressing room. She'd given up trying to insist on a more conservative dress. So, among the classic black, she had a shimmering silver sleeveless, a Christmas red made of a slinky material, a white trimmed in gold sequins, the leopard print that she agreed to try on although she knew she'd hate it, and last but not least, a royal blue in crushed velvet.

Every time she walked out of the dressing room to model for Katherine, Katherine would gasp. "Oh my. You look stunning."

Maggie had lost a few pounds since the whole Trey thing had started. She didn't do it on purpose, but with a nervous tummy occurring most of the time, she found herself eating smaller portions and less often.

She'd saved her two favorites for last. The silver metallic sleeveless and the basic black with bell sleeves.

Katherine thumped her chin with her finger and pursed her lips. "I like that one on you, Maggie." She turned her around, eyeing her entire silhouette. "I wasn't too keen on the black, but the sleeves are flattering on you."

Maggie crossed her arms, her nostrils flaring. "Is that another way of saying a good way to hide my batwing arms?" Maggie pouted.

"No! You're in great shape…"

"For an older woman. I don't know what I was thinking! I can't possibly go to New York to be with

Trey. It's the most ludicrous thing I've ever heard." She marched into the dressing room to change.

"Maggie, you're beautiful, and I didn't mean anything by that. I just thought the black dress highlighted your best features. You looked stunning in it."

Just then Maggie emerged from behind the door with all the dresses. "Here, help me put these away."

"I won't put this away because this is the one you're going to buy and wear to the New Year's Eve dinner with Trey." She dangled the black dress, daring Maggie to cross her.

Maggie chuckled. "Okay, maybe I'm being a bit sensitive." She grabbed the hanger out of Katherine's hand.

Katherine slid her arm over her friend's shoulder. "Now, let's go look for sexy negligées."

After an exhausting afternoon of shopping, the two women found a café and ordered lunch.

"Did he say where he's taking you?" Katherine's gaze hung above the rim of her coffee mug.

"No. He just said he got a hotel downtown."

Katherine giggled. "I'm so envious."

"Why?"

"New love is so exciting," Katherine said, her cheeks flushing.

"I know," Maggie said, leaning in. "I don't know what the heck I'm doing."

Katherine leveled her stare. "Please. It all comes back very naturally. Like riding a bike."

Maggie shrugged. "What if I'm not pretty enough. I mean I have wrinkles, and I've had a child."

"Maggie Regan! He knows all of that. He must be attracted to you regardless. He doesn't want some Barbie to date. He wants a real woman." She forked a chunk of lettuce, bringing it to her mouth.

"True. Why do you think he's remained single so long? Maybe he has some odd quirks I haven't seen yet."

"You mean like belching at the table, or maybe passing gas while watching television, or no wait, scratching his...well, you know."

"Katherine!"

"Well, don't be so silly, Maggie. I'm sure he's not perfect, but what man is? If he makes you happy in all the right places"—her eyes danced—"then don't worry about the small stuff." She opened her mouth and devoured the bite of salad.

Shaking her head at her crazy friend, Maggie took a bite of her salad too.

"Thanks for taking me shopping today. Whenever I need a reality check, you're my go-to person." Maggie opened the car door, pulling her bags out with her. She leaned in. "I'll call you before I head to the airport."

"Have a great time, Maggie. I can't wait to hear all about it."

Maggie shut the door and stepped back. Katherine flashed her a wave and sped off.

Surprisingly, Collette was completely on board with Maggie's little escape to New York. Wow, how times had changed. She'd never in a million years think she'd ever be jet-setting to New York for New Year's Eve, let alone spending the weekend with another man. But she'd never in a million years think something would take her Richard away, either.

She finished packing and rolled her suitcase out to the living room. Thankfully, Collette had one she could borrow. She switched on the television, tossed another log onto the fire, then walked over to the kitchen to start the water for tea and hunt for something to eat. In the other room, the special report interrupted the programming on the television. She stretched her ear to listen.

The weather report showed a severe winter storm heading from the Midwest toward the East Coast. The blizzard-like conditions concerned her, but she tried to remain positive.

~

*P*icking up the phone, she called Collette. Was she really traveling to New York to be with a guy who'd she'd only met just a short time ago? The phone rang in her ear.

"Hey, Mom. I was just thinking about you," Collette said.

"I'm heading off to the airport," Maggie told Collette.

"Have a great trip, Mom."

Then she called Katherine. "I'm heading off to the airport."

"I've been thinking about this day! You have a blast."

"Have you seen any weather reports?" Maggie sandwiched the phone between her head and shoulder as she struggled to put on her jacket.

"Yeah, looks like a storm coming. You two will be snuggling. Don't let a little cold weather and snow spook you." The bold laugh Katherine exuded made Maggie giggle.

Maggie finished putting on her winter attire, then headed to the car. The drive to the airport left her feeling like she was floating on a cloud. She parked her car in the long-term parking lot, then made her way toward the airline check-in. She vaguely recalled getting there, but once she was amid the hundreds of people traveling through the security checkpoints, reality set in. She unloaded her coat, scarf, and shoes and tossed them into the gray bin on the conveyer belt along with her purse. She waited her turn to go through the security scanner and once through, re-dressed and hurried to her gate. Tired from the rigmarole of security and a little scared overall about her trip, she found an empty seat and waited for the announcement regarding boarding.

She noticed they hadn't updated the board for a current departure time to her first layover in Houston. From there she was going to Chicago O'Hare then to JFK. She got up and stretched her arms and legs, then hunted for a bathroom. After she did that, she went in search of a couple of magazines and a cup of coffee.

She'd just made her way back to the gate when they announced the delays. Thirty-five minutes wasn't too bad. She could still get her connection in time out of Houston.

Once she boarded the plane to Houston, she flipped through her magazines, had refreshments, and dozed a little.

Getting to Houston brought her that much closer to Trey. She hurried to the next gate that would take her to Chicago. She drooped her shoulders. "Not another delay." She sighed, then her gaze darted around the packed terminal. Not a single empty chair. She walked to the next gate and found an empty seat and sat, keeping her ears turned toward her gate to hear any updates. Here she was worried about missing her flight out of Houston, and it might be the Chicago one she misses.

And just like the flight out of Eugene, her flight out of Houston was late, but once she boarded the plane, she could breathe a sigh of relief. She knew that a winter storm was barreling down on her, and she wanted to get to New York before it did. It seemed the airports were being extra cautious, and it hadn't even happened yet.

When she landed in Chicago, she called Trey.

"It's good to hear your voice. How have the airports been?"

"Terrible. Delays, delays, delays," she said.

"Well, you're almost here, and I can't wait to hold you in my arms."

A warm, tingly feeling overwhelmed her with hearing his voice anyway, but when he spoke the words of endearment, it left her absolutely tongue-tied. She savored every word.

"Wait. They're making an announcement." She craned her ear toward the sounds. The plane was going to be delayed overnight due to mechanical issues.

"Oh no. I'm going to be late."

"What did they say?"

Trey's alarmed tone gave Maggie comfort in knowing he cared. "Mechanical issues. Overnight. I'm stranded in Chicago!"

"Damn. Are they giving you a time for tomorrow?"

"No. Just to check with the airline before coming back to the airport. So, I guess I'll catch a cab to a hotel."

"I'm so sorry, babe."

She arched her brows. This was new. He'd never called her that before.

"I know. It's messed up as the kids would say." She laughed at herself.

"After you get settled into the hotel call me."

"Okay, Trey. Talk to you soon," she said as she

slowly made her way down the halls of the airport and out into the streets of the Windy City.

She hailed a cab, and with no luggage, told the driver to take her to the hotel that the airline staff had suggested. After she got checked in, she purchased a toothbrush, toothpaste, and a small travel-size deodorant. Thankfully, she had her makeup kit and a hairbrush in her purse. She was going to do her best to look good when she fell into Trey's arms the following day.

She draped her clothes over the chair to minimize wrinkling and took a long, hot shower. She climbed into bed naked, something she never did, but figured it was the best solution since she'd have to wear the same clothes the following day. She prayed there'd be no fire or other natural disaster, or if one came, it took her out lock, stock, and barrel so that she'd never know the embarrassment of being buck naked in a strange hotel room and having to explain it all.

She snuggled down deep under the covers and with the only light in the room flickering from the television, she called Trey.

"I was beginning to worry about you," he said.

There came the warm thoughts of concern again that totally made her day. "I'm fine. Except I don't have any luggage."

He laughed. "No clothes, huh?"

"Nope. I'm sleeping with no clothes on." Her hand flew to her mouth when she realized how that might sound.

"That sounds pretty interesting," he said in a low, gravelly tone that set her tummy to doing flip-flops and somersaults.

"This has been an adventure for sure," she said, changing the subject.

"Sleeping naked?"

"Trey, I'm trying to change the subject here. Work with me." She laughed.

"You mean the delays and all. It's par for the course. Seems holidays always equate with winter weather for the East Coast. That's why I dread coming back this way during Christmastime."

"I did it for you. I did it because you asked me to. I don't usually go off to strange places with strange men." Feeling sleep come over her after an exhausting day of travel, all she really wanted right now was a comfortable bed.

"Hey, I'm not strange." His low belly laugh made her giddy.

"I'm tired so I think I'll get some sleep. I'll let you know how things go tomorrow."

"I can check on things here. They update the

website with departure times. If I find out something before you, I'll call you."

"Trey?"

"Uh-huh?"

"You called me babe. I liked that."

She checked out of her room, but with time to kill, sat in the hotel lobby until almost four p.m., taking a cab back to the airport where her seven-p.m. flight would finally take her to JFK. Trey promised to be at the airport to receive her. She boarded the plane and closed her eyes. It would be a quick jaunt to New York, but maybe if she rested, it would go by even quicker. She just wanted to be in New York and be with Trey.

She made her way to the baggage claim area where she located the carousel her baggage would come on. After about fifteen minutes, the dark blue suitcase with the bright red bow on the handle, an idea Collette gave her so she could easily identify her bag, came rolling by. She carted it off the carousel and made her way outside. She had no idea what he'd be driving. They forgot to discuss that part. She walked up and down the side-walk, pulling her suitcase along, trying to keep the night chilled air off by buttoning up her jacket and securely fastening her scarf around her neck. The wind was brutal, and snow was coming down in buckets.

"Maggie!"

She turned toward the voice. There, Trey—waving like a madman—stood outside the driver's side of a dark sedan. She quickly made her way toward him. He moved around the car toward the trunk and popped it open. He took her bag and tossed it in. Then he slammed the lid shut and leaned in for a kiss. His lips were icy cold.

He gently eased her mouth open and teased her with his tongue. The kiss made her head heavy. She stepped back.

"I'm so glad to see you." Her eyes filled with water.

"Babe. Why the tears?" He took her hand and led her to the car.

"It's been such a trying trip. I'm just happy to be here." He opened the door and helped her in.

"You're here now, and that's all that matters." His eyes sparkled, making her stomach pitch and roll.

The traffic getting out of the airport was a total nightmare. Trey mumbled a few chosen words as he maneuvered among the honking cars. After they got out of the congestion, they both calmed down and were able to talk a little.

"I hate New York traffic as much as I do San Francisco," he sneered.

"I do too. I don't miss this at all."

"Once we get to the hotel, we won't leave until it's time to go back to the airport."

She could feel her cheeks turn warm and wondered if he'd noticed her blushing.

"Aren't I going to meet your parents?"

"I don't know. Tomorrow is New Year's Eve, and I have something special planned. You're heading home on the second."

"I messed things up. I'm sorry." She lowered her gaze and fiddled with her hands.

"It's not your fault. It's the weather." He reached over and laid his hand on hers.

She enjoyed the warmth of his hand. She turned her attention out the window. She'd spent over half her life in New York, and yet now she was seeing it with fresh eyes.

~

Trey concentrated deeply as he maneuvered his way toward the hotel. He casually glanced over to her a couple of times, watching her as she took in the city. He couldn't tell if she was smiling or not, but every now and then she'd make a small noise or gesture that made him think she was enjoying the views.

"We're just minutes from Rockefeller Center, Radio City Music Hall, and Saint Patrick's Cathedral," he said.

She whirled her head around. "Lotte Palace?"

He nodded.

"Trey. That place is so expensive."

"It's New Year's Eve. And, you've come a long way. It'll be fun."

She clasped her hands in her lap and focused ahead. "What do you have planned," she asked.

In a low voice, he said, "I don't have anything special except for dinner tomorrow night. I've made reservations at one of the most romantic restaurants in all of the city."

She rolled her head toward him. Blinking a couple of times, she tossed around a few restaurants in her mind she knew to have that title. But then she gasped when she remembered one. "Are you taking me…"

"Now, Maggie. Let me have one surprise, please," he said, lowering his tone even more.

She leaned back into the seat paying attention to what was going on outside the car. "It's hard to surprise me. Remember, I lived in this city for a good many years."

"I know, but I want this to be about us. We're making memories here this weekend."

She quickly glanced back at him, her cheeks full-on burning up. "Trey."

He put on his blinker and turned the car down Madison Ave. "Yes," he said, peering up and out as he tried to locate the entrance to the hotel.

"It's been a long time since I've been romantically involved with anyone."

The car ambled along the circular driveway. "Here we are."

"Here we are," Maggie echoed.

"Don't worry, Maggie. I'll never do anything you don't want me to."

Just then the valet opened the car door for Trey and welcomed them to the Lotte Palace. Another employee grabbed the bags and rolled them inside to the lobby on a luggage cart while Trey checked them in.

"Yes, we have reservations today. Trey Simmons."

The clerk went to work checking the computer, taking a credit card from Trey and after charging his credit card, handed him keys. When he turned around, Maggie was standing back out of the way. She hunched her shoulders then took steps toward him.

"We're on the tenth floor." He handed her a plastic card.

She rolled it over in the palm of her hand. "I don't need my own key."

He pulled his neck back and studied her through half-closed lids.

She handed him the key. "We can share a key," she said.

He cupped her hand and pushed it back gently. "No, we have separate rooms. This is your key to your room."

Her lips stretched sideways. "I knew that. I'm sorry. I don't know what I was thinking. It must be jet lag." She pulled her hand away and gripped the plastic card.

They made their way toward the elevator.

"After you," he said, motioning for her to step inside first.

The ride up to the tenth floor was expeditious and fairly quiet. One would expect only the best at the Lotte Palace. With its thirty-foot Christmas tree in the courtyard, to the festive decorations in the lobby, the Lotte New York Palace was known for exceptionalism. The doors to the elevator slowly opened.

They walked down the beautifully carpeted hall and found their rooms. "We're right next door to each other." He stepped toward one of the doors. "Your luggage should already be inside. Let's meet out in the hall in about twenty minutes? We can go exploring." He unlocked his door and stepped inside.

~

Maggie inserted the keycard and opened her door. Once inside the room, she checked out her accommodations. Decorated with the most beautiful pieces of furniture, Maggie ran her hand along the quilted bedcover. She peeked in the bathroom. Marble floors and shower, mirrors trimmed and gilded. She sighed. Towels so plush her hand sank in deep when she touched them, and a matching white robe hung on a hook. She walked back out to the main room. Her gaze went the wall where an adjoining door was. She shook her head. Nothing was going to happen that required a secret passageway to Trey's room.

When her phone began to ring, and she saw it was Collette, she answered it.

"Mom?"

"Yes, hon. I'm here. I finally made it."

"Good. I've been concerned."

"I'm sorry. I should have called you sooner. We're at the hotel. I was just freshening up."

"I…"

Maggie realized it may have come off like Collette had interrupted them. "No, we have separate rooms. I was just freshening up because we're going out in a bit."

"Mom! Too much information." Collette laughed in her ear.

Maggie dropped down to the corner of the bed and crossed her legs at the ankle. "This is just all so awkward for me. I feel I may have made a mistake."

"Mom, we talked about that. You're just having some fun. Don't do anything you don't want to. Just enjoy yourself. And, if he pressures you in any way, you take a cab to the airport and wait for your flight or see if you can change it."

"I doubt I have to go through all that. I'd just go to another hotel anyway. But besides, he's in his room, and I'm in mine. What could possibly happen?"

CHAPTER 11

Trey put his toiletry items out on the counter in the bathroom. He hung up his clothes, set his shoes along the wall, and flipped through the hotel guide. It had probably been about fifteen minutes. She would be waiting for him in the hall. *Maybe I should have booked just one room.* He shook his head. *What kind of person would she think I was to just assume she'd share a room with me?* He closed the suitcase and stepped back. He would want nothing more than to share a room, share his bed with her, but that would be presuming an awful lot. They weren't kids though. They'd both been in love, had to deal with loss, depression, and everything that comes with losing someone you love. He drew on a jacket, wrapped the scarf around his neck, and pulled on a knit cap. He picked up the black leather gloves and shoved them inside his pocket, then moved toward the door. His gaze went to the door in the wall as he quickly exited the room to step outside where he found Maggie waiting.

"Ready?" he said with a gleeful expression.

"Ready as I'll ever be."

He offered his arm for her. She laced her hand through and off they went, chattering about what beautiful accommodations they had.

~

It was a very cold evening. The kind where you could see your breath. She huddled as close to him as she could without giving signals it was anything more than just trying to keep warm. Sure, they'd kissed, and well, steamy ones at that. In fact, she couldn't remember the last time she kissed Richard like that. Maybe while they were dating, on their honeymoon, maybe the first few years of their marriage? She shrugged off the silly thoughts and held Trey closer.

They moseyed down Madison Avenue window-shopping. The sidewalks were crowded with out-of-towners and tourists getting ready for the party of the year. They tipped their heads, acknowledging those who passed them by. Some were couples holding hands, others were singles out to have a good time.

Trey stopped in front of a little establishment. Music and laughter bellowed from the walls and door. "Shall we go inside and get something to drink?"

"Yes, I'm freezing. I can hardly feel my toes."

Trey opened the heavy black door, and she stepped inside first. Squinting, she gingerly moved, getting used to the darkness of the room. A young blonde woman came up to her.

"Two? Follow me, please."

Maggie followed with Trey close behind. The young woman led them to a booth in the back. Music filled the space, and along with the loud talking, it was hard to hear your own voice. Maggie slid into the booth and began to pull off her outer garments. She peeled the scarf off and slipped out of the heavy jacket, finally tossing her hat on top of the pile. She shrugged.

"It's toasty in here," Trey said, following suit with undressing from his winter wardrobe.

They ordered hot buttered rum drinks and an appetizer to share.

"It's almost ten," Maggie said, trying to conceal her yawn behind her hand.

"I bet you're exhausted."

The way he looked at her made her breath catch in

her throat. "I'm a little tired, yes," she managed to squeak out.

"After we have our drinks we'll head back. I thought we'd go have breakfast tomorrow, then maybe do some ice skating, shopping, then we'll go out on the town and see the New Year in." He acknowledged the waitress as she served them. He waited until they were alone again. "To a great weekend with the most beautiful woman on earth."

Maggie held her mug next to his and clanked it. "Trey, you always know the right things to say." She pulled the glass cup away from his and drew in a taste of the warm, sweet beverage.

He reached across the table for her hand. She slowly slid it to him where he laced his fingers with hers. He rubbed imaginary circles on the palm of her hand, right below the thumb, sending shivers up and down her spine.

"I haven't had a pair of ice skates on my feet in years," she said, trying to break the sexual tension she felt coming on.

"We can do something else," he said, low and steady.

She swallowed hard. What on earth did he mean by that? Stay in bed all day eating chocolate-covered strawberries? *That's ridiculous. Strawberries aren't in season.* She shook her head. *Well of course they can be in season for the Lotte Palace hotel.* Now she was screaming in her head. Thankfully no one else could hear her rambling thoughts.

"What do you have in mind?" She fluttered her lashes.

"How about we just take it slow and easy, do what comes naturally. We won't plan a thing." He squeezed her hand.

She drew in a deep breath and held it. Slow and easy. Yikes.

~

*A*fter they finished their drinks and late-night snack, the two headed back to the hotel. He held her hand snugly, and with a light swing in their step and arms, trotted down the sidewalk.

"I'm so happy you are here," he said, pulling her hand and arm up to his chest.

"I am too. It's sort of out of my comfort zone, though." She peered up at him.

"Mine too. But it feels so right."

"We don't know each other, though, Trey."

He stopped. Putting both hands on her shoulders, he turned her toward him.

She drew in her bottom lip and bit down.

Pinching his expression, he said, "Will you stop saying that, please?"

"Well, it's true. Think back. I come out to the park to see you paint, twice. I invite you in for tea and cookies, twice. We walk the paths deep into the woods, we go to another park for a picnic lunch, and now I'm in New York City spending the weekend with you. I'd say that equates to not knowing someone very well."

He held her hands, hesitating briefly before continuing. "True. Everything you say is true. But we share a connection. Your husband and my fiancé were killed. Here in this city. Do you think it was just a mere coincidence that I drove to Eugene where you moved to, only to meet you and find this out? No. I should say not. It's fate, Maggie."

His dreamy expression melted into determination as he pulled her in, first for a hug, only to find her mouth and kiss her. He devoured her mouth with deep, sweeping strokes of his tongue, leaving her breathless and dizzy with desire.

He pulled back, still holding her. "Do you believe in fate, Maggie?"

She removed herself from his hold and stepped back. She inhaled deeply before answering, letting the cool air fill her lungs. "Yes, I do. I think you found me for a reason."

The hunger in his eyes made her knees wobble and her pulse quicken.

"I. I—" she began.

He put his finger to her mouth to silence her. Then he leaned in and kissed her.

CHAPTER 12

"Hey get a room!"

Maggie broke the kiss and peered over Trey's shoulder. A group of rowdy young people who'd been enjoying the festivities a bit too much waved at them from across the way. Trey slipped his arm around her shoulder, and they began to walk back to the hotel. "Kids," he said under his breath.

"They're just having fun." She wiped the wet flake off her cheek. "It's snowing!"

The white stuff began to come down softly at first, then turned to a steady stream, forming a soft layer on the streets and sidewalks. As the snow flitted down, a soft, warm glow from the streetlamps exaggerated the snowflakes, making them appear larger and more abundant than just mere wandering particles of ice water.

She laced her arm through Trey's. She calmly watched as he braved the weather and snow, his head slung low as he collided with wind and cold. She laughed.

"What's so funny?" His words came out like puffs of clouds.

"You've lived in San Francisco too long. You've forgotten about our winter wonderland." She squeezed his arm.

He cupped her hand. "It gets cold in San Fran, but it's more about not seeing the sunshine until noon because of the fog."

"I couldn't handle that. I have to see the sunshine or I'm a mess."

"Maybe that's my issue." He pulled her arm inward, then laughed a hearty one, making her giggle.

"Tomorrow when we wake up, there will be a blanket of white over everything."

"Perfect day for a carriage ride," he said.

Stomping their feet to get off any powder, they entered the grand hotel lobby and made their way to the elevator. Once they got to their floor, Maggie's pulse quickened. This was the part she dreaded. Did she ask him to come in her room, did she bat her lashes a few times inviting him to kiss her, or did she quietly but pleasantly thank him for a nice evening and hurry into her room. Alone.

"Well, here we are," he said, motioning to their doors, side by side.

"Here we are," she echoed. She pulled off her scarf and held it.

"Breakfast tomorrow?"

"Sounds great," she said, lowering her gaze.

"I'm never sure if women eat breakfast. I know I have to have something in my stomach at the start of the day or I'm a big, bad bear."

"This woman eats breakfast, lunch, and dinner." She patted her round hips.

He reached for her and pulled her close. "I love your womanly figure. It's what makes you so sexy." He dropped a kiss on her forehead.

She held her breath.

"Seriously. Stick-thin women are not for me. Give me a real woman any day of the week."

She let out the held breath slowly.

"Aren't you going to say anything?" He rocked her in his arms, setting a fire deep in the pit of her stomach.

"What can I say? You embarrass me, but at the same time, you make me feel as if I'm the only one on this earth. Like we're floating around attached somehow, and everything you say is great."

He lowered his head and kissed her. She kissed him back.

"Well, guess I'll see you in the morning," he said, letting go of his hold.

She walked backward a couple of steps, and when her heel hit the door, she turned around. She inserted her keycard and opened the door. "Good night, Trey."

"Good night, Maggie."

~

*H*e closed the door to his room and pulled off his cap and scarf. She aroused him in every way possible and getting her out of his mind would be hard to do tonight. His gaze focused on the door that kept them apart. The one in the wall that adjoined the rooms. He stepped over toward it, raising his fist to knock. He thought better of it and quickly stepped back. *What would I say? Hey, can I come in for some more hot kisses? Or how about, I can't fall asleep tonight without kissing you one last time?* He shook his head while kicking off his boots. He threw himself on his bed and crossed his arms behind his head. Looking at the ceiling, he thought back to his engagement to Lacy.

They had a love connection that he'd never experienced before. The way she touched him set his emotions ablaze, and when they were together it was like a freight train barreling down the tracks, or a bull in a china shop. It was hot, it was lustful, and it was something that mere words couldn't describe. And when they weren't making love, they were just as passionate about their work, their life after work, and their families.

Maggie was so different in every aspect. But he was a different person now too. And Maggie...she was all he could think about. He closed his eyes, recalling the softness of her hips under his fingers, the softness of her lips and her face. He knew all too well she felt insecure because of their age difference, but he loved every little laugh and brow line, and her laugh was worth a million dollars. He pulled up off the bed and went to take a shower. But as he passed by the lonely door that separated them, the urge and desire to see her one last time pulled him in like a vacuum. He knocked twice.

~

She couldn't sleep. How could she? The man she yearned for was right behind that door. She thought about his caress, the way he moved, setting off fireworks she'd not felt in a long, long time. The way he pulled her in and stared at her before he kissed her. It quickened her pulse every time. She swung her legs off the bed and sat straight up. The yearning to go knock on the door overcame her. She walked toward the door, balled her fist and started to knock when a tap followed by another jolted her momentarily. She gasped.

"Yes," she called out.

"It's me, Trey."

She giggled. "Of course, it's you, Trey. Who else would it be?" She palmed her forehead thinking about this strange conversation she was having with a man on the other side of this door.

"Can I come in?" His voice was muffled but his intentions clear.

She unlocked the door and opened it.

His stare took her breath away for the fourteenth time that day. But who was counting? He stood in stocking feet with his shirt untucked and his hair a bit disheveled, looking so darn sexy all she wanted to do was pull him in and kick the door shut.

"Maggie," he said.

She nodded.

"I can't stop thinking about you. I want you so badly. I haven't felt this way about anyone in so long."

The forlorn look covered his face and like a magnet, drew her right in. She walked toward him.

He held out his hands. She took them and held them tightly.

"I can't stop thinking about you, either. I mean what is it we're doing?"

He pulled her in and found her mouth, devouring her lips. She raised up on her toes and slid her hands around his neck, running them through his hair. He groaned, then he did what she thought about doing. He kicked the door shut.

CHAPTER 13

Who could even think about food at a time like this? They'd walked down to the hotel restaurant and soon were seated by a window. Branches that were free of leaves now were covered in snow, and the streets which were once dry were covered in a slushy substance from all the cars driving on the roads. But in the distance, you could see mounds of the white stuff and the gray sky told the story that more of the same white snowflakes would be coming down later.

They sipped on coffee while looking at the menu. Maggie wondered what he was thinking about. Did she live up to his standards or his expectations for that matter? She studied the menu hard. She glanced over everything, but nothing made total sense. Eggs. She'd order eggs. Oh, and toast. That would be a good choice.

"Maggie," he said, looking over his menu.

"Yes." She dropped hers down so she could see his dazzling eyes.

"What are you in the mood for?"

Her heart skipped a beat. *In the mood? Are you serious?* "Eggs. Toast," she whispered.

"I think I'll have an omelet."

They ordered their breakfast, avoiding the awkward state she found difficult to maneuver around.

He reached out his hand to her, and she graciously took the gesture as a way to break the awkward silence. But he just stared at her for seconds, saying nothing at all. She swallowed hard, squeaking out a few words.

"The snow is so pretty, isn't it?" She nodded toward the streets.

"I think a carriage ride is in definite order today. I wish I'd brought my paints. Talk about a scenic moment." He shook his head.

Now they were making progress. "If memory serves me well, I believe there's an art store not too far from here. What do you say we go shopping?"

"I don't know," he said, trying to scoff at the idea.

"Trey, it would be awesome to see you paint a scene

from our time here this weekend. Please," she said, begging.

After breakfast, they sought out the store, and sure enough, Maggie's memory did serve her well. Trey purchased a sketch pad instead of a canvas and some sketching pencils instead of paint and brushes.

"I didn't know you also sketched. What else don't I know about you?" She arched her brows.

"Probably more than you care to know. You know the important stuff."

They made their way to the carriage stop on the outskirts of Central Park and purchased tickets for a ride. Huddled under a blanket, they toured the city from their perch in the white, glossy carriage while sipping on hot chocolate topped with tiny floating marshmallows.

"So, you want to know everything about me, huh?" He sneaked in a kiss.

She smiled, bobbing her head like a yo-yo.

"I grew up in a two-parent household. For the most part, I'd say it was normal, or average at least." He chuckled. "I went to law school, and while there I met the girl of my dreams. Lacy." He lowered his gaze to her mouth.

She tipped her chin and motioned him to go on.

The carriage clonked through the park.

"Anyway, I met Lacy at the library, and we started a conversation that led to…well, you know the rest." He pointed to kids tossing snowballs.

"But what about after her and 9-11?" She placed her hand on his knee, sending a wave of pleasure through his limbs.

"I became celibate for a good many years. I never even looked at another woman."

She shot him a weird look.

"I know. It's hard to believe." He palmed his chest.

She knocked shoulders with him. "Be serious, Trey."

"I am. I didn't date, I didn't look at women, I just kept my focus on my work."

"When did you finally let someone in?" she asked.

"I let my guard down and went out with one of the law clerks in my office. That didn't work out so well. She just wanted sex."

Maggie blushed and giggled.

"Then one of my buddies set me up with a friend of a friend sort of thing. That lasted about three dates. When I discovered she had marriage and kids on her mind, I was like heading for the hills." He laughed.

"Kids aren't so bad," she said.

"I know, but I'm not interested in having any. I'm too old anyway. I do want a dog, though."

"So, you've basically been working for the past seventeen years and no social life to be had?"

He shook his head. "Nose to the grindstone. That's me. Now, what about you?"

~

She studied his serious face. She pursed her lips as she combed her vocabulary for the words.

"I'm sure you've had guys falling at your feet, right?" He laid his hand in her lap. And although they had a blanket between them, she could feel his body heat radiate through it. She shivered.

"No. I sort of followed your path. I dated a little, but the truth of the matter is, no one could compare to my Richard. I got tired of always sizing them up, and I think they got tired of me always starting most of my sentences off with, "When Richard and I…"

"You don't do that," he said, his low and gravelly tone making the hairs on her arms stand up.

"I know. I think it's because when I finally realized I needed to come to grips with being a widow and all that it entailed, I also grew in my own strength and independence. So now I can start off my sentences with, "I'd like to do this, or do that."

"I can see that. I never for once thought you were anything but a strong, independent gal." His smile shot right through her, sending waves of admiration for her to muse.

"I've enjoyed the solace living in the country has brought me. I've gotten to know myself better. And although I loved Richard with all my heart and never would have wanted such a tragedy to occur— for anyone—it made me grow up really fast, and it also had me searching for what was important in life. I'd love to have Richard back in my life, grow old with him like we planned, but it wasn't in the cards, I guess," she said, her voice wavering.

"Like I said earlier, if you believe in fate, then you must believe in us." He searched under the blanket for her hand. "I love being with you, Maggie. You've made me whole again." He pulled her hand to his lips and kissed it.

His kisses warmed her entire body. Savoring every moment, every touch, she couldn't imagine being with anyone else. They were destined to be together. She knew it, and now she'd given in to it. And with no regrets either.

She'd been through hell and back, and so had he. It was time to put the healing to the test and see if their two broken hearts could be mended once and for all. She held his hand to her mouth, relishing in the softness of his touch.

"Maggie, I've been thinking a lot about us."

"I've been thinking about us too."

"How can a long-distance relationship work?"

"It would be very hard, but we can do it. I'll visit you in San Francisco, and when time permits, you come to Eugene."

"That sounds all fine and dandy now, but I bet that gets old quickly."

"I've waited seventeen years for you. I can wait a few weeks or months." She snuggled closer to him, lifting her chin for the kiss. The kiss she wanted so badly.

He lowered his mouth to hers and gave her what she wanted. What she needed. What she craved.

The carriage came to an abrupt stop. The driver began to ring a large brass bell.

Trey jumped out and held his hand out for Maggie to take. He took hold of both her hands and eased her down to the sidewalk.

"That was so much fun," she said, holding his hand as they walked.

"So, what's next on the agenda?" He stopped and studied her face.

"What time is the special dinner tonight?"

"We've been having so much impromptu fun, I almost forgot about my surprise. Reservations are for seven."

"We can just sit and people watch. I don't know if you've noticed, but New York has plenty of interesting folks."

"Okay, but first, I must sketch something." He held up the white plastic bag from the art store.

They made their way toward a bench. Sitting side by side, Trey went to work on some secret project. Whenever she leaned over to take a peek, he pulled it away from prying eyes.

"You have to wait. Just a little bit longer." He turned his back, his broad shoulders blocking her view.

She made a *humph* sound, then playfully smacked him on the shoulder. She watched as families strolled with babies in carriages and dogs on leashes. She nodded to the young couple snuggled close as they walked by. Finally, after about twenty minutes, he turned back around.

"Close your eyes."

"Close my eyes?" She obeyed.

"On the count of three open them."

Her eyes flew open on three and went immediately to the pad he held. A penciled carriage with horses and in the background a tree-lined sidewalk replicating the park. She gasped. "You are so talented." She took it from his hands so she could admire it up close.

"This would be a beautiful painting, Trey."

"I was thinking the very same thing." He stood.

"I should have brought my camera. I didn't even think about it."

He took her hand, and they walked out of the park toward the hotel.

"We'll have other opportunities to take pictures. I'm not going anywhere." He squeezed her hand.

"Trey. Do you think people are laughing at me?"

He stopped dead in his tracks and faced her. "Why on earth would you think that?"

She lowered her gaze.

He tipped her chin upward with his finger. "Seriously. Why would you say that?"

"Older woman robbing the cradle."

"Maggie Regan. That's the most ridiculous thing I've ever heard of. Besides…" He pulled her in by the shoulders, his mouth mere centimeters from hers. His sweet breath mingled with hers. "Age is just a number. I've been told I'm just an old soul anyway, so see, it works."

"Are you calling me old?" She smirked, then smiled.

He kissed her nose, then found her mouth. "All I know is, everything my friends have said about older women is true!"

She slapped him on the arm, laughing off the remark.

"See, there's my feisty girl." He hugged her and then dropped a kiss on the top of her head.

~

They slowly walked up to their perspective rooms, holding hands and smiling like two lovestruck teenagers. Trey pulled out his phone and studied it for a second. "So, let's see. I know women take a bit longer to get ready, so…" He chuckled. "I'll pick you up at six thirty. It will take us that long to get across town."

"I'll ignore that little part about taking longer to get ready." She leaned in and kissed his warm lips.

He held her tight, not letting her move away. She peered up through her lashes and arched her brows. "What?"

"I love the way you feel in my arms."

She nodded. "I admit it does feel pretty good."

"Pretty good?" He pulled his head back and frowned.

"Pretty good like women take longer to get ready?" She palmed his chest and laughed.

"I see how it is." He began to tickle her, making her laugh harder.

"Trey, stop," she pleaded.

The two stood in silence, focused on each other, each breathing a bit harder from all the flirtatious play. Maggie chewed her lip and held her breath, trying to steady her nerves, but the look in Trey's eyes made her feel tingly. Before she realized it, she moved closer to him, right into his arms. He leaned down and found her mouth, kissing her softly at first, then with more intent and desire. She welcomed his passion, and when she began to feel dizzy from all the senses that traveled through her body, she released her hold and stepped back.

He brushed his hand along his chin, his eyes heavy with desire. She blinked a few times. "I better go inside and get ready." She turned toward the door and fumbled for her keycard.

He laid his hand on hers and didn't move it. She didn't want to turn around or look up at him because she knew it would only mean trouble for her. Trouble in a good way. She could feel her heart racing a mile a minute and her body temperature rising just as fast. She took a slow breath. Finally finding the courage to face him, she looked him straight on. He took the keycard out of her hand and inserted it for her. He opened her door and pushed it open wide. She stepped inside, turning to face him. She held out her hands to him, and he waltzed right into them. She was angry at herself for falling for him and his sex appeal, but she also knew she might not ever get a second chance of love and happiness, and despite age just being a number, she wasn't getting any younger. She thought about the black lacy negligée for a fleeting moment. There would be no time for that today.

~

He held her a moment too long perhaps, but he didn't want her to go. In his arms, he held her captive so he could kiss her. She had to feel it too. When they joked and it broke the ice…the hotness of their kisses, it gave them both a minute to gather their senses. But hell, all he could think about was her in his arms, his mouth on hers, and the softness of her touch. When she opened her arms to him, it was if he was on autopilot. His mind, body, and soul knew just what to do.

He closed the door, and when he turned back around, he found her with her arms wide open. He'd finally found happiness. They were destined to be together. He stepped into her arms, taking in the fresh scent of her. Stepping back but still holding her, he reached up and touched her cheek. "Maggie," he said.

"Yes," she whispered.

"I want you to know that I respect you in every way. I don't want to pressure you into anything you don't want to do. I can wait." He trailed kisses down her neck.

"It's a little late for that, isn't it?"

Her comment struck a chord. He released his hold on her and stepped back.

Maggie knitted her brows. "Did I say something wrong?

Trey lowered his gaze and studied the design in the carpet.

"Trey," she whispered. "Did I say something to change your mind?"

He drew in a deep breath. "No. You didn't do a thing wrong. I think it's me." He turned his back and made his way toward the door.

"Trey, don't go. Let's talk."

He stopped.

"Maybe we're moving too fast. I'm not going

anywhere. Isn't that what we've been saying to each other. I'm sorry if I made you feel…"

Her tone sounded pleading, and it annoyed him a bit. Talk about mixed signals. He took another step.

"No, wait. I'm not sorry. I'm confused."

He whirled around.

"I'm not sorry for feeling this way with you. I'm not sorry one single bit." Her gaze darted all over him. "I love being with you, Trey. You make me feel young and worthy."

He swiftly moved to her and pulled her in. "You're a beautiful woman, Maggie. I think about you nonstop. It's probably not healthy how much I think about you." A small sound, part grunt and part laugh, escaped his tight lips.

"Then stay." She moved her hands around his neck and pulled him down for a kiss.

CHAPTER 14

He clasped her hand and playfully led her down the long, carpeted hallway toward the elevator. She tried to keep up while putting on one of her shoes. Her hair still damp from the shower flopped down her back. Catching her breath while they waited for the elevator, she tossed her hair up in a twist and secured it with a pretty clip she'd bought just for the occasion.

"I probably look like a hot mess." She took out her small compact mirror and studied her face.

"One hot mess, all right." He pulled her in and kissed her neck.

"Trey." She giggled.

The doors flew open. An older couple, probably in their seventies stood in the elevator, not smiling a bit.

Trey took Maggie by the hand and moved into the space.

"Good evening," he said, nodding to the gentleman.

"Good evening," he replied.

The older woman stared Maggie up and down.

"New York is so fabulous this time of year," Trey said, trying to break the awkward feeling.

Maggie squeezed his hand.

The doors flew open. "After you," Trey said, motioning to the couple.

Once they stepped out, Trey and Maggie followed, laughing and running toward the valet counter to fetch their car.

"Did you see the way they stared at us?" Maggie shook her head.

"They were just jealous." He sneaked in another kiss.

Once the valet brought the car around, Trey helped Maggie into the car. "I think I forgot to tell you how beautiful you look tonight. That dress is something else on you." His gaze traveled the length of her body, making her squirm just a tad.

"Thank you. You look rather dapper yourself." She winked.

He drove a little fast through the streets of New York. It was the holiday season, dinnertime, and for some, quitting time after spending hours at the office. He maneuvered the lanes and even ran a few yellow lights. It was New York. Everyone ran lights.

He pulled up to the door of the restaurant and got out. He handed the keys to the valet and helped Maggie out. "Welcome to one of the most romantic restaurants in all of New York—One if by land, Two if by sea."

Maggie raised her brows, then took his hand. She didn't have the proclivity to tell him.

The host sat them at a wonderful table and gave them a few minutes to look over the menu while they waited for the server.

"This restaurant has a rich history. Started off being Aaron Burr's carriage house." He studied the menu. "It has a tunnel underneath as well." He stopped short of finishing his sentence. "You've been here before, haven't you?"

She clenched her jaw tight, then nodded. "A few times."

"I should have known," he said, dropping the menu.

"Trey, it's okay. I'm here with you making new memories."

"Everywhere we go in this city we'll be reminded of our past. Who am I kidding?"

She reached out and clutched his hand. "Did you think that we'd be able to hide from our past?"

He mouthed, "No."

"This is a perfect way to end our stay here. Well almost perfect," she whispered in a sexy tone.

He squeezed her hand. "You're right. So maybe we need to go to another state and make new memories. Just for us?"

"We are. In Eugene. In San Francisco."

"I'll be drawn back here because of my parents."

"And that's all right. And, for Lacy and Richard too."

He shot her a puzzled look.

"These people were important to us, Trey. We can't ignore it. Tomorrow I'm going to take you someplace, okay?"

They ordered dinner and enjoyed the rest of the evening, and instead of avoiding talking about Richard and Lacy, they embraced it. Maggie felt so much freedom from that night.

Finishing up one of the most exciting New Year's Eves she'd had in a very long time, Trey and Maggie entered the hotel's restaurant and bar where a celebration was underway. They were handed party favors—hat, horn, and an embossed champagne glass with the hotel's name, and year, and led to a table for two. They danced to the live band, drank way too much bubbly stuff, and ate some delightful appetizers. When midnight came, they ushered in the new year with a sweet kiss and danced some more. With her feet killing her—she'd not worn heels in quite some time—Trey convinced her to kick them off.

"She did," he said, motioning toward a young blonde who'd clearly had too much to drink.

"She can get away with it. She's young and dumb." Maggie took another sip of her bubbly drink. "I'll just sit here awhile."

They sat holding hands and giving each other dreamy looks. When a slow song came on, Trey jumped up and pulled her out to the dance floor. When the level of desire got a bit too much, she pulled apart. "Am I a bad person for feeling…"

He leaned in and kissed her. "No, I'm feeling it too." He whirled her around, pulling her back in for another kiss.

After that dance, they called it a night even though several couples they'd befriended during the evening tried to convince them to stay for the breakfast buffet the hotel was throwing as part of the package.

Maggie was just as happy about skipping the breakfast. Her feet were killing her, and when Trey promised to rub them, well, who needed bacon and eggs?

As they walked the long hall that led to their adjoining rooms, Maggie reflected on not just this evening, but every moment before. She turned her head slightly and studied his profile. He turned and caught her looking and leaned over and kissed her.

"Did you have a good time tonight?" he asked.

"Yes, I did. It was magical. I feel like we're starring in some Hallmark movie," she whispered, then squeezed his hand.

"Speaking of Hallmark, did you see the one about the lady who designed the dating app?" His boyish grin made her giggle.

She nodded. "I love all of the Hallmark Christmas movies."

"Well, here we are," he said, leading her right up to her door.

She slipped her hand inside the small, silver sequined evening bag Katherine had loaned her and retrieved her room key. "I don't want tonight to end, Trey." She tilted her head back and focused on him.

"I know. But we have a busy day ahead. You said you had a surprise for me?" He sported another boyish grin.

"True. But you said you'd rub my sore and very tired feet." She pouted her lips and batted her lashes.

He took her card out of her hand and inserted it. With one push, he opened the door, ushering her through. She tossed her bag and coat on the chair, then slipped off her shoes.

"I was only teasing. You don't have to rub my feet. Just getting those off," she said, gesturing toward the high-heeled shoes, "is good enough for me. A long hot soak in a tub will do wonders. I'll be good as new."

"I'll start running your bath now." He took off toward the bathroom before she could protest.

She sat on the edge of the bed listening to the water fill the tub, picturing him standing in the bathroom with only a towel on. She leaned back on her arms, tilting her chin toward the ceiling. *Maggie, Maggie. Get those thoughts out of your head right now.*

"All ready for madam," he said, bowing.

"Trey, you're so funny. Thank you for thinking of me. I hope you sleep well." She walked him to the door.

"I'll sleep like a baby. You know why?" He took both of her hands in his.

She laced her fingers with his, and while watching his eyes, an uncontrollable thump pounded. She shook her head slowly. She thought she knew why, but she wanted to hear it from his lips.

"Because I've spent the best weekend with someone that is special to me. I hope you feel the same way about me."

"I do, Trey. I really do. I think we have some unfinished business though." She hated to be the killjoy in this magical moment, but someone had to keep it real.

His eyes widened, then his jaw dropped. "Unfinished business?"

"You'll see. Tomorrow." She raised up on tiptoes, closed her eyes, and kissed him.

"What time are we going to your surprise tomorrow?" He made his way to the secret door between their rooms.

"After breakfast sometime. We'll take a cab."

He turned the knob and opened the door. "See you then." He stepped into his room and began to pull the door close.

~

*M*aggie called and made arrangements for the cab to pick them up at the hotel. She asked Trey to just trust her and go with it. When the driver pulled up to let them off, Trey's look of sorrow bled through. They held hands as they made their way through the memorial site.

They gazed at the twin reflecting pools and listened as the water rushed from the largest waterfalls in North America. The pools sat within the footprints of the Towers and just being there made her skin prickle.

They worked their way toward the bronze panels that edged the pools where every name of every person who died in 2001 as well as in the 1993 World Trade Center attack was memorialized.

Trey released his hold of her hand and began to search the wall for Lacy's name. Maggie started on one end to look for Richard's. This was a big step for each of them. She'd never been able to bring herself to visit the site. She'd tried to stay as far away from New York as she possibly could. In a way, she was punishing the city when it wasn't their fault. Richard and she loved New York. But she loved Eugene, Oregon, now.

She moved along the wall, reading the names. She stopped, and her jaw dropped when she found it. Her gaze darted in and out of the sea of people visiting the wall, trying to find Trey. She held her breath when she spotted him. With his head bowed, he rested his hand on Lacy's engraved name.

Maggie turned her attention back to Richard's engraving. "There's so much I want to tell you," she said, closed mouth. Shrugging, she turned her attention to Richard's name. "Collette is doing well, and we have a beautiful grandson, Sam." A tear rolled down her cheek. Should she tell him about Trey?

Her gaze traveled down to Trey who was still holding on to Lacy. She hoped she'd made the right decision bringing him here. She wiped away another stray tear that dribbled down her face. She drew in a deep breath and just studied Richard's name harder and longer. Finally, she whispered, "I'm finding happiness, Richard. It's taken me a long time, but I'm finally there. His name is Trey. I'm the older woman, can you believe that?" She chuckled. "He makes me happy, and I need that. I've been alone for so long. I'll always love you, but now I've made room in my heart for another. Rest in peace." She shoved off from the wall and with her head down, she made her way to Trey.

She stood back, not crowding him. She wanted him to take all the time he needed. She'd said her piece to Richard. She didn't feel the need to ask him for permission about Trey. She only wanted to let him know she was finally at peace and happy and that maybe now he could rest too.

Trey signaled her with his index finger extended. "A few more minutes."

"Of course. Take your time." She spotted an empty bench. "I'll sit over there," she said, motioning toward it.

She sat and crossed her legs. She fiddled with a loose string on her scarf, then tucked her hands in her jacket. Despite wearing gloves, she was cold. Just then a snowflake hit her on the eyelash, causing her to blink.

Her eyes moved upward. Plop, another one hit her on the eyelid. She giggled. Then the flurries came down fast and many. They must have caught Trey's attention, too, because he turned away from the wall and found Maggie where she said she'd be.

She patted the space next to her for him to sit.

He groaned when he sat.

"Are you okay?" She laced her arm with his.

"Yes," he said with a sigh.

"It's hard to come here, that's for sure. But I'm glad we came."

He quickly craned his neck toward her, his eyes full of question. He wrinkled his brow. "You've never been here before?"

She shook her head. "First time."

He reached for her hand and held it. "Me too."

She nodded.

"Did you know I've never been here before?" His puzzled look returned.

She cupped their hands. "I figured as much."

He leaned in and kissed her. "Thank you for bringing me here. I think it's what I needed to move on."

"I don't expect you to tell me what you said over there"—she tipped her chin toward the wall—"but I would like to share with you what I said to Richard."

He stood, lifting her up with him. "No, you don't have to."

"I want to. It should explain a few things, like my behavior last night. I told him I'd been alone for a long time and that I'd finally found happiness and his name was Trey. I told him I'd always love him, but that I've made room in my heart for you." Her eyes began to mist, and along with the many flakes of freshly falling snow, she was covered in melted snow and water from her tears.

"I told Lacy that I was sorry for the miscommunication that day. That it wasn't supposed to work out that way." His speech choked. He cleared his throat. "But I told her I knew she didn't blame me, that it was the dumbass terrorists that did this. Not me." His eyes began to mist again.

"Trey, Trey," Maggie said, pulling him in for a hug. "She knows that. There's no way she'd ever blame you. You loved her with all your being."

He sobbed quietly, then brushing away the tears, he shook off his sadness and straightened his back. "I feel free. I really do. I did what I've been dreading, but now that I've gotten it off my chest, I feel so much better."

"Good." Maggie moved her hand up and down his arm, rubbing it lightly.

"I also told her about us. I told her that I'd met

someone who made me happy and I lived to see your smiling face." He held her hand on his arm, then pulled her in for a hug. "I do love you, Maggie. Maybe you don't want me to say it, but I feel it within every inch of my being. You make me laugh, make me cry, make me want to stay in bed all day, and you light up my life."

"I love you, too, Trey. I wanted Richard to be the first to know how I felt. I know that may sound strange, but I felt like I was cheating on him. I mean, I know I'm not, but it's just this feeling."

He lowered his mouth to hers and kissed her.

"You also make me want to get up every morning and see what the day has in store for me. I enjoy our walks, talks, and all the quiet moments we share." A wistful countenance heated her face. "I'm starving. What do you say we grab a hotdog from the old man over on the corner and head back to the hotel?" She led the way.

CHAPTER 15

They hugged, kissed, then hugged some more. Why were goodbyes always the most melodramatic at the airport? *I must go. I really must. But before I do, one last kiss. Oh. Do I have to go?* And on and on it goes.

"I don't want you to leave," he whispered in her ear, sending chills down her spine.

"I have to, Trey." She closed her eyes, savoring his woodsy scent and relishing his strong hold.

"When can I see you again?" He held her in a tight embrace.

"I don't know. We haven't discussed that. Maybe I can come to San Francisco for a visit?" She stepped out of his hold and readjusted the strap to her shoulder bag.

"I think I better get in that line." She nodded to the long line for security.

"Maggie."

Maggie whirled around.

"I meant what I said. I want you to know that."

Her jaw hung wide open, then she quickly drew it close. Well of course he meant it. Didn't he? "I know you did, Trey." She blew him a kiss and hurried to get in line. She counted to five before she searched for him, but a sea of travelers blocked her view every time.

The plane trip home was uneventful, thank goodness. She didn't need any upsets regarding travel to pile on top of the now very out in the open May-December romance she had going on with Trey. She shook her head, then a slow, cautious smile curled up on the corners of her lips. Why shouldn't she be relishing this? She wasn't getting any younger, and she was so tired of being alone. But maybe this wasn't the answer. After all, Trey lived in another state.

~

Trey entered the parking garage and located his car. He called his folks to let them know he was on the way to their house. They had dinner plans, and his mom wanted to see Christmas lights even though it was the new year.

They had dinner at an Italian restaurant a few blocks from their house. Then his dad drove up and down streets so his mom could ooh and aah over decorated lawns and houses. Trey tried to act interested, but now that the holidays were over, all he could think about was Maggie. Sweet, sweet Maggie.

"I was hoping to meet your new friend," his mom said as she gazed out the car window.

"I was too. It just didn't work out. She had weather delays, so we only had a little time to be together. Next time," he said, looking at his phone.

Few words were spoken the rest of the evening. Trey mentioned stopping at a coffee shop for dessert.

"Thank you for coming home for Christmas, Trey. It meant a lot to us," his mother said, looking over to his father.

Trey's dad had just taken a bite of a giant chocolate chip cookie. Wiping his mouth with a napkin, he nodded. "Yes, good to see you, Son."

"It was nice to be in New York again. Unfortunately, my flight leaves early tomorrow. I need to get back to the hotel."

"I don't know why you just don't stay the night with us," his mother said.

"I told you. The hotel is closer to the airport. I'd already booked it." He slid out from the green leather booth and stood at the end of the table. He held his hand out to his mother to help her out.

As they pulled up to his parents' house, his mother asked the question he knew was coming. The one that came every time she knew he was about to leave.

"Can you come in?"

"No, Mom. Have to head back downtown. I'll call you when I get back home."

The look of sadness in her eyes could get to him, but not this time. He gave his mom a hug and shook his dad's hand, pulling him in for a hug as an afterthought. "Thanks for everything." He walked around to his car and just as he opened the car door, he peered at them over the hood. They both were standing on the stoop, huddled. He threw up one last wave and got in his car and drove away.

~

With the phone plastered against his head and staring at the ceiling, Trey called Maggie. When she answered out of breath, her throaty and sensual tone shot through him like boiling water.

"Hey, babe."

"Hi, Trey. How was dinner?"

"Good. I thought about you all night long. I'm thinking about you right at this moment too."

She chuckled into his ear. "Tell me more."

"The carriage ride brought back some memories."

She laughed again. "It's freezing here. I just brought in a load of wood."

Trey shifted his body. "That's why you need me there. To help chop and load wood." He puffed out his chest, emphasizing the strong guy stance.

"Haha. I've been chopping and stacking my wood for a long time, Trey. Thank you very much."

"Yes, but don't you want me to be the one to help you?" he toyed with her and loved every minute of it.

"Trey Simmons. You're messing with me. When are you coming back?"

"I don't know. I have to be at work day after tomorrow. I get in around dinnertime tomorrow night. As much as I will miss you, I can't wait to sleep in my own bed."

"Call me when you get in. I'll be thinking about you. I better toss on a log or my fire will burn out. It's barely sparking now."

"Okay, Maggie. I'll let you go, but only until we meet again."

"You are so romantic, Trey Simmons."

Maggie lifted the fireplace screen away and tossed in two medium-sized logs. The loud snap, crackle, and pop made her pull her head back. She hurriedly repositioned the screen. After making a cup of Italian coffee in honor of Trey's Italian dinner, she sat on the couch and stared at the dancing flames. Mesmerized by their color and the sounds of the fire, Maggie pictured Trey lying in the big bed all alone. She grabbed her arms and gave herself a hug. She closed her eyes and tried to remember what his strong arms felt like—how his warm mouth trailed up her neck, giving her goose bumps. She tossed her head back and snickered. *Maggie Regan. You should be ashamed of yourself.*

CHAPTER 16

She tried to keep her mind busy on the day-to-day details of life rather than dwelling on him. It was harder to do than she expected. In between keeping the cold, wet winter at bay, Maggie also took long walks when the sun decided to come out and visited Collette and family, and Katherine. It was good for a few minutes or even an hour of actively engaging her mind with small talk and other mind-busy tactics, but when it was the end of the day and it was just her, Trey always came creeping in.

During one of these such moments of mind-busying tactics, Katherine had invited Maggie out for a night on the town. Maggie, dressed in jeans, boots, a warm jacket, scarf, and knit hat, met Katherine at a local café that was known for wood-fired pizza and great glasses of wine or local draft beer.

She waved at Katherine from the door, then made her way to the pub table where Katherine was already enjoying a glass of red wine. She kissed Maggie on the cheek.

"You look great. How are you?" Katherine beamed ear to ear.

"I'm good." Maggie pulled herself up to the high stool and sat. The dimly lit restaurant had several empty tables. "It's rather quiet in here tonight." She picked up a menu and eyed the listing.

"They'll be coming in here before long. You know the college kids. They eat late."

Maggie laughed. "I think I'm going to have a bambino Italian sausage with onions and mushrooms." She closed the menu. "And a glass of pinot." She tipped her head, satisfied with her choice.

"Sounds delicious. I think I'll have a bambino pepperoni—and a glass of zin."

A young man, approximately twenty-something with black-rimmed glasses and dark blond hair with broad shoulders, came over to get their order. He was cute in a Superman, Clark Kent sort of way.

After he left the two women giggled. "Why am I noticing all these young guys now?" Katherine smirked.

"Don't blame me," Maggie said, shaking her head. "Besides, you're happily married."

"I know. I can look, though can't I?" She laughed.

The server brought over their wine. When he walked away, Katherine proposed a toast.

"To my best friend in the entire world. I'm so happy for you."

"Ditto," Maggie said, clanking her glass with Katherine's.

"So, tell me all about New York."

"Well, I've already told you a lot over the phone. We had a great time. We bonded." Maggie played with the rim of her wineglass.

"Great time doesn't tell me squat." Katherine drummed her fingers on the table.

Maggie knew what she wanted, and she in no way was going to give her *those* details. "We had a lovely dinner, we went on a carriage ride, we strolled along the sidewalks in freshly fallen snow…"

Katherine held up her hand. "Stop right there. I got all of that. But what about you two."

Maggie cocked her head and raised her brows. "We came to a great understanding. We're going to be okay."

"Maggie Regan. Are you not going to tell me just a little bit of what it was like being with him?"

Maggie glanced around the restaurant and nearby

tables. She didn't want any witnesses to what she was about to share with Katherine. She leaned forward with her elbows on the table. She popped her finger open beckoning her to come forward. "It was the most exciting thing I've felt in a long time. I'd forgotten about how it feels to be tangled up under the sheets, or how a touch can be so moving. Or how hours of kissing can chap your lips. I must have gone through two tubes of lip balm." She pulled her head back, a small beam curling up on the corners of her mouth.

Katherine, still leaning over the table, closed her mouth. She sat up and grabbed a napkin to wipe the drool. "I'm so jealous." She shook her head, and taking a long gulp of her wine, slumped into the seat.

Maggie chuckled. "I tried not to tell you, but no… you wouldn't let up. So, there you go. Now, try going to sleep tonight knowing that little tidbit of information."

"When do you see him next?"

Just then the server brought their hot out of the oven wood-fired pizzas.

"I'm not sure. I hope soon." Maggie sprinkled on some parmesan cheese and red pepper.

"How do you think this long-distance relationship will work out?" Katherine pulled one of the slices away from the pan and set it on the provided small plate.

"I don't know. But I have a plan that might have him staying right here in Eugene."

~

Maggie sat in one of those plastic waiting room chairs. She nervously picked at her nails as she tried to go over in her head everything she wanted to convey. This might be her only shot.

When her name was called, she bolted straight out of the chair and made her way toward the soft-spoken woman standing. Maggie extended her hand and introduced herself.

"Maggie Regan," she said.

"Hello, Ms. Regan. Please," the lady said, motioning toward the open door.

Maggie stepped inside the sparsely furnished office and found another plastic chair to sit in. *What would you expect for a national park office? Mahogany desks and leather chairs?*

"Let's see," the woman said as she sat behind her gray metal desk. "You're here to discuss the old covered bridge out at Hope Creek."

It seemed strange to hear this person speak about a park that was literally right across the street from the house she'd been living in for over seventeen years. Maggie nodded.

The woman, who was dressed in green slacks and a top with the National Park Service emblem sewn onto the pocket, sat back in her chair and peered over her wire-rimmed glasses. "What exactly did you want to talk about?" She clasped her hands and moved them onto the desk.

"It's in disarray. It needs some maintenance. I know funds are tight within the park service, but I was wondering if maybe I would be able to take on the preservation of the bridge myself." She flashed a warm smile toward the woman sitting across from her.

With her mouth slightly ajar after hearing what Maggie proposed, she promptly closed it. "It's not unheard of. You know, private citizens taking on a project such as this." She leaned back in her chair. "You realize it could be quite costly."

"I was hoping to have a partner and also do a lot of fund-raising. I think that bridge could draw a lot of visitors to the park. I live right across the street." She beamed.

"Oh, I see. Then you have a ventured interest in preserving it."

"Yes, I guess I do." Maggie tipped her chin.

"I need to get approval, and there will be plenty of

documents to sign if approved." She slid her chair back. "I'll be in touch." She walked around the desk.

Maggie shook her hand. "Thank you so much for seeing me today. I look forward to your call. Hopefully, we'll be able to work it all out."

"So, Ms. Regan, to be clear, you want the bridge to remain in its current location. You'll work on it from there?"

"I think that's the perfect place for it. But I think we need to spruce up the park some, make it more of an attraction to get people to come see the bridge."

"It is on the covered bridge map. There's not a lot else we can do."

"Signage, I don't know. I'll think of something," Maggie said, strumming her chin with her fingers.

On the way home, Maggie thought long and hard about her ideas for the bridge. She knew that if she could raise enough money, they could fix the bridge up. There would be no moving costs associated with the refurbishment, so that was a definite plus. But what could Maggie do, if anything, to bring more awareness to the bridge?

*M*aggie pulled the casserole from the oven and leaned over, taking in a deep whiff of the dish. Closing her eyes, she drew in the wonderful aroma that wafted about, making her mouth water. She opened the small pot where green beans simmered. She tossed in the foil packet of rolls and began to set the table. Collette, Jeremy, and Sam were coming over.

A knock on the door followed by a loud hello made Maggie peer around the corner. "Come in, guys," she called out.

"Something smells so good," Jeremy said.

Sam jumped up and down, and rubbing his tummy with his hand, he licked his lips and said, "Yum."

Collette took off his jacket and tossed it over the back of the nearby chair. "What can I help you with?"

"I've got everything under control. Maybe get the glasses down and fill them with water?"

Collette crossed over to the cabinet and retrieved the glasses, and from the water dispenser of the refrigerator, began to fill them. While she was doing that, Maggie pulled the plates off the table.

"Let's dish this up to cool." Maggie handed Collette a large serving spoon.

As Collette dished up the chicken goodness as they

nicknamed it, Maggie spooned green beans on each plate, setting them back on the table. The rolls came out last.

They said grace before chowing down, and then for a few minutes, it was silent except for the occasional chewing sound.

"Sam, chew with your mouth closed," Collette said.

Blushing for being called out, Sam lowered his head.

"It's okay, Sam. Just remember to close while chewing," Maggie said, trying to soften the reprimand. That's what nanas were for, right?

"Collette tells me you met with the park service regarding that old covered bridge." Jeremy took a bite of his food and chewed.

"Yes, I'm very hopeful they'll honor my request. I want to refurbish the bridge. You know it has a name, right?" She locked eyes with Jeremey. "Not just the old bridge." She laughed as she forked the casserole

Jeremy raised his brows.

"Hopeberry. Hopeberry Bridge at Hope Creek."

"What year was it built?" Collette asked.

"1920."

A small grunt escaped Jeremy's mouth. "That's right up there with some of the oldies."

"I went to the library to dig up as much information

as I could on Hopeberry. Seems there may have been a pretty little gal named Hope that lived nearby. The wild berry bushes that grow in the woods were also inspiration for the name. I think we could put that place back on the map."

"Mom, be careful what you wish for. Putting that bridge on the map could mean tons of people visiting. Thought you liked the quiet out here," Collette said.

"I did. I do," Maggie said. "But it gets rather lonely out here sometimes. It would be nice to hear children laughing, people having a good time. I need something to do with my time." She thought about Trey and their magical moments together. She shook her head. "You know… to be productive as I go into my golden years."

"Mom, that's a long time from now. You are so young at heart."

Young at heart. She wondered if that was code for your wrinkles don't matter because you're young at heart. She sneered. "I know, but…so to change the subject slightly…I'm headed to San Francisco for a few days." She lowered her gaze, not prepared for the wide-eyed look Collette no doubt would give her. The clatter of silverware dropping made her look up. "Did I say something wrong?" She forked some of the chicken goodness and plopped it into her mouth.

CHAPTER 17

The two women cleared off the table while Jeremy stoked the fire and Sam played with a LEGO set. Maggie filled the sink with hot water and squirted some soap to make bubbles. Collette scraped the dishes and set them in the sudsy water. Maggie busied herself by putting leftovers in containers for them to take home, keeping just a little for herself. She would be leaving for San Francisco the day after tomorrow.

"Mom," Collette said, scrubbing the plates, then handing them to Maggie to rinse and dry.

"Uh-huh," Maggie said, stacking plates on the counter.

"Is this serious with you and the painter?"

Maggie sighed. "What is it with you young people.

Things and people have names. Hopeberry Bridge, and Trey. Trey is his name." She reached up on her tiptoes and slid the plates onto the shelf.

"Trey. Is this serious with Trey."

She shrugged. "I think it is."

"Why are you hiding it from me?" Collette wiped her hands on the nearby towel and crossed her arms.

"I'm not. It's just new, and I don't know how to go about it." Maggie relaxed her face as she studied her daughter's features. She was the spitting image of Richard.

"That's cool. You don't have anything to be ashamed of. If that's what you're thinking." She began washing dishes again.

"Not ashamed. No. I guess I just never thought I'd be starting over at this stage of my life. I thought I'd grow old with your dad."

Collette turned to look at her mom while her hands were still in the suds. "Ahh. That's so sweet, Mom. I know Dad would want you to be happy."

Now she was the spitting image of Richard.

"So, how long are you going for?"

"Just a few days. I don't like to be gone from the house that long."

"Why? You don't have any pets. Stay as long as you

like." Collette play bumped into her shoulder, making her blush.

"I already got my return ticket. But I'm sure I'll be visiting him again."

"Good. The next time he comes to Eugene, let's all get together and have dinner."

Maggie drew in a deep breath and held it. She wasn't sure she was ready for all that. "We'll see, dear." She dried the silverware while looking out into space.

~

He paced the sidewalk, waiting for her to come running out of the doors and into his arms. Every time he thought he saw someone that resembled her, he held his breath. Finally, she came out pulling her small suitcase behind her. He wrapped his arms around her and holding her back slightly, dived deeply into her eyes. "Hello, Maggie." He dropped his mouth to hers.

He pulled back briefly, but when she flashed her award-winning grin, he couldn't resist. He went in for another kiss. This time a longer one.

"Hello, indeed," she said.

He gave her a quick pat on the back, letting his hand move to her arm. "I've been waiting for this day."

He popped the trunk open, tossing her suitcase in, then ushered her into the passenger side of the car. He dropped into his seat, breathing heavily. "It's so good to see you." He clasped her hand in his.

"I'm happy you're happy to see me." She winked.

"Happy is not the right word. But I'll take it." He leaned over and kissed her.

He loved her style, but the way she felt in his arms was even better. He pulled back, staring at her.

"What? Do I have something on my face?" She ran her hand along her cheeks and mouth.

"No, I'm just staring at the most beautiful woman on earth." He beamed.

As they drove through the city to his apartment, they chatted. He laughed when she commented on the traffic.

"It's like this on most days. Stop and go all the way." He looked to the left, then darted into the other lane, speeding up, trying to make better time. He couldn't wait to be alone with her.

"I live right downtown. Walking distance to many great restaurants. So, I thought we'd just find something around there for dinner. What are you in the mood for?" He knew what he was in the mood for, and it wasn't food. "Chinese? Mexican? Sushi?"

"Hmm. All of it sounds delicious," she said. "Wow, some really narrow and hilly streets here."

They drove for about twenty more minutes before he pulled into a large, covered parking area.

He held her hand and pulled her suitcase with his other. Once inside the apartment, he told her to make herself comfortable and wheeled her suitcase into the bedroom. He quickly checked to make sure nothing was out of place. He peered into the bathroom, and everything appeared tidy, complete with fresh towels. He met her in the living room where he found her sitting on his couch.

"Are you tired?" He sat next to her and slid his arm around her, pulling her close.

"Not really. It's a short flight here."

"True." He grabbed a remote off the table. Flames danced from the wall-mounted fireplace. Then he turned on music with another remote.

"Wow. All the modern conveniences, huh?" She patted his leg.

He covered her hand with his. "It's San Francisco. What can I say?"

$\mathcal{M}$aggie knitted her brows. The apartment didn't seem to suit him, but as he said, it was San Francisco. He always enjoyed chopping the wood and stoking the real fire. The stark furnishings of the room made her feel a bit uncomfortable too. But the warmth of his hand on hers made a lot of her uneasiness fade.

"Trey?"

He leaned in and began trailing warm kisses up her neck. "Uh-huh," he said in a low, gravelly tone.

She leaned her head back and closed her eyes, feeling the heat building up within her body. "I went to the park service and inquired about saving the bridge."

He moved up to her mouth and covered it. She moaned softly, then she laced her hands around his neck and ran her fingers through his hair. She'd tell him later about Hopeberry.

~

$\mathcal{N}$either of them had an appetite, but even Maggie knew that one could not live on love alone. Maggie grinned when she thought of him in her arms. They walked hand in hand to the nearby

Chinese restaurant Trey frequented. They ordered lemon chicken, shrimp fried rice, and eggrolls.

"Tomorrow we can go get seafood down at the wharf if you want." He leaned in and kissed her.

"Sounds great. So, where did we leave off?" Maggie poured them each green tea in the delicate china cups.

"Let's see, I said…"

Maggie gasped. "No, not then." She blushed. "I was telling you about the bridge." She could feel her face burning up.

"Oh, that." He winked.

Maggie heaved her shoulders and let out a deep breath. "Can we be serious just once?"

"I'll try, but when you look at me like that, I can't concentrate." He cupped her hand and squeezed it, sending shivers up her spine.

She wondered if this is what she'd be dealing with if they became a true couple. Attention deficit disorder. "I have a great idea about Hopeberry."

"Hopeberry?"

The way his gaze traveled her face and other parts of her body made her squirm. They were not going to get any business done tonight. She slumped. "The bridge," she mumbled.

"I'm just teasing. I know it's the covered bridge." He

sat up straight and clasped his hand on the table. "Tell me. I'm all ears. But hurry." He grinned.

She told him all about her visit and how she saw the future of the bridge. He was a great listener, only nodding and shaking his head when necessary. When she was finished, he leaned in.

"I think you're a genius, Maggie Regan. Raising money, hiring locals to help restore it, and making it a showcase for weddings and other special photo ops. I mean, it's just great. It's quaint enough that it will draw a lot of people, but not big enough to have everyone searching for it. If you put it in some wedding brochures, it will end up being busy enough. Couples love to get married outdoors and especially have their wedding and engagement photos taken outdoors."

"I can see families at Easter, during the holidays… the ideas for that bridge are endless." She drew in a taste of her tea.

"I think you've fallen onto something, and it's going to be great. I want to be a part of it too." His eyes twinkled.

She tried to read his eyes, his expression. Was he saying what she thought he was saying—what she hoped he was saying? "I'd love for you to be part of it. After all, I don't think I would have ever given that old bridge a second thought if I hadn't met you at the park that day." She held her breath as her eyes journeyed to all areas of his face. Her pulse quickened, and the hairs on her arms stood.

He nodded slowly. "I don't want to be apart from you any longer. I've been thinking long and hard about this decision. But I've made it."

She leaned back and swallowed hard, waiting for him to continue.

"I'm going to give notice to the firm and move to Eugene."

Her lids flew open, and she gasped. "Seriously?"

"If you'll have me."

"Oh, Trey. Of course, I'll have you." She reached out her hand.

He laced his fingers with hers. "I love you, Maggie Regan."

A small tear rolled down her cheek. "I can't believe this is happening to me." She closed her eyes.

"Believe it. Believe it with all your heart."

She opened her eyes. And yes, he was still there holding her hand.

CHAPTER 18

After her short but very satisfying weekend with Trey, Maggie headed back to Eugene where she told him she'd get the ball rolling regarding her ideas for the restoration of Hopeberry Bridge. She'd not been this enthusiastic about anything for a long time. She sat at the table, staring at her legal-size pad. She strummed the table with her pencil while she thought about things she wanted to jot down. She picked up her mug and sipped the warm tea. She'd let it sit too long and now it was barely drinkable. She liked her tea hot. She scooted her chair out and made her way to the microwave. As she watched the turntable go around, an idea popped into her head. She dashed to the tablet to write it down before it left her. Darn senior moments. They were happening more and more.

Maggie's computer was a dinosaur. She hadn't used it for years. She'd been meaning to get rid of it, but out of sight out of mind. She lugged the small gray box out to her car and sat it in the trunk. She then made a trip to the computer store.

When she got up to the customer service counter and repair desk, the clerk, a young man probably in his twenties with a tattoo of a skull on his hand, grunted when she lifted the computer up onto the glass counter.

"That's an oldie," he said.

"Yes, I've had it for a long time. I don't even know if it works. Can you add some stuff to it to make it more up to date?"

The guy laughed and stepped away from the counter and crossed his arms. "No way. That thing is older than dirt. You need a new one. That processor is so out of date."

"Okay, then can you point me in the right direction for a new one?" Maggie said.

"The salesman will help you." He motioned with his head over to an aisle nearby.

"Can you dispose of the computer for me?" Maggie asked, holding on to any shred of dignity she had.

"For twenty bucks."

Maggie furrowed her brows. "It will cost me twenty bucks to get rid of it?"

The young man nodded.

Maggie drew out a twenty-dollar bill and slapped it on the counter.

"It's called a waste removal fee," the young man said as he rung up the transaction on the cash register.

"Thank you," Maggie said, walking away and trying to find a salesman.

She made eye contact with a fellow that had a name tag on that read Paul. Paul came up and asked if he could help her with something. She paused a moment as she didn't want him to think she knew absolutely nothing about computers, although she didn't. She'd read about how salesman liked to take advantage of women. Especially older women.

"I'm looking for a computer."

The man laughed. "You've come to the right aisle then," he said, resting a hand on a computer.

Maggie fidgeted with her purse. So much for acting halfway intelligent about the matter. "Something mid-priced, mainly to type documents and send email." She walked up to one and eyed it as if she knew what she was looking at.

"Do you need the monitor too?"

She rose up from reading the details about the computer and stared at him. She didn't think to bring her old monitor too. It was probably outdated as well. But she'd save herself the waste removal fee and just dump it herself. "I suppose I do."

Paul walked down the aisle to an endcap. She followed him.

"This is a great deal. You get the computer and monitor as a package deal."

Maggie studied the price tag. It seemed reasonable. "Okay, I'll take it."

The man was nice enough to give her a quick lesson on how to set it up. Maggie made her purchase and headed home.

After she set up the computer and monitor, she had to get down on the floor to hook up all the cables. She blew a piece of hair that had fallen into her eyes out of the way so she could see the connections. She bumped her head at least twice on the underside of the desk, and when it was time to crawl out from under it, she got a charley horse in her leg. She hardly ever drank, but this called for something stronger than tea. She slowly made her way to the kitchen.

As she sipped on the amber liquid, she also rubbed her poor leg. It took her by surprise, that old charley horse. The drink warmed her up, and soon she didn't feel any soreness from struggling with computer cables or anything else. Her cell phone began to vibrate on the table.

"Hello, Trey."

"Hey. How are you?"

"I'm not sure you want to know."

"Of course, I do," he said.

"I bought a new computer. Apparently, my old one was made during the ice age."

A low belly laugh radiated through the phone. "That's pretty old."

"That's what the kid said behind the counter too. But I bought a new one, got it all hooked up. Glad you weren't here to see that. It wasn't pretty." She laughed.

"I can't imagine anything you do not being pretty."

She closed her eyes and listened to his soft voice flattering with compliments. It was enough to make her blush.

"You're so kind. But after I bumped my head on the underside of the computer desk and said a few choice words, I was punished with a bad cramp in my leg. I figured I'd already made the powers that be angry, so I had a scotch. And it wasn't on the rocks."

"Oh, wow. I wish I could have been there to help you. Sounds like you've had a rough day. You need me to be there to rub your feet and calves."

The last time he rubbed her feet they fell into bed. "I wish you were here to do that as well. By the way, when are you coming here?" Her tone was smooth as glass and as velvety as the amber drink she'd just consumed.

"That's why I called. Besides to say hello to my beautiful woman. I gave my notice, and everything is set. I had to sweet talk my landlord out of the lease. But since apartments are hard to come by here, he let me out without taking my deposit. So, looks like in about three weeks I'll be there to hold you in my arms."

Holding her in his arms. That sounded too nice. "I can't wait," she said.

After her conversation with Trey, she took a hot bath to soak that sore leg and the other limbs that called uncle during her recent activity. She laid her head back against the porcelain tub and closed her eyes, letting the hot water heal and rejuvenate her. Looking like a prune from staying in the water too long, she dried off and put on her comfy pajamas. Then she sat at the new electronic device and powered it up. She spent the next two hours downloading software and setting up her email account. She sent Trey an email to try it out. In a matter of minutes, she got a message that popped up down in the corner of her monitor. She just received her first email.

What are you doing up still? Playing with your new toy? I can't wait to hold you. I miss you so much.
Trey

She pounded out a quick reply.

That's twice you mentioned you can't wait to hold me. I love it when you make me your top priority. I miss you, too.
Maggie
Good night my love. Sleep tight.
Trey

I don't know what I did to deserve you, but I'm happy you're in my life. I love you.

Maggie

Then she got a reply back with a smiley face and a big red heart. She sat back and stared at the last message. She didn't know what she did to deserve him. She shook her head. She powered down the computer and turned off the monitor. She made her way to the kitchen for one more little sip of that scotch she saved for special occasions. Then, she slept like a baby.

*L*ike a soldier on a mission, Maggie grabbed her purse and keys and marched out of the house on her way over to Katherine's. She promised to help her organize the very first, but surely not last, fund-raiser for Hopeberry.

"Tea?" Katherine called out from the kitchen.

Maggie undressed from her heavy coat and scarf and hung them over the chairback. "Sounds delicious and warm."

"I know, right? I'm ready for spring," Katherine said, setting a mug of tea in front of Maggie.

Maggie held the cup in her hands to warm them up. She closed her eyes and breathed in the lovely aroma of rose petals and cinnamon. She slowly raised the mug to her mouth, testing the heat and blew on the hot beverage.

"So, I've been thinking a lot about fund-raisers," Katherine said.

"Good. That's a very good thing." Maggie tipped her head back and forth.

"The Scouts love projects. It helps them earn badges, right?" Katherine said.

"True," Maggie said.

"We ask them if they'd be interested in sprucing up the area first. The bridge is overgrown with all kind of vegetation. Then, we can have a paint party. That's probably worth at least three badges." Katherine sat back in her chair with one leg curled up under her bottom.

"I like those ideas. We'll need someone or a few people to volunteer to make the bridge sound again. There is a lot of dry rot going on. And a new plaque. Someone in the signage industry. The Girl Scouts love bake sales too. So maybe we could have some sort of function at the park with music and a bake sale. I want to get the public involved somehow." Maggie jotted down the ideas on the pad she brought.

"I'll reach out to some of the troops in the area and report back to you," Katherine said, making her own notes.

"I'll contact a local sign company and also see about someone handy with tools that has experience with refurbishing a bridge," Maggie said.

"That's a specific skill set. You might have trouble

locating a someone who can refurbish a bridge." She cackled at her statement.

"I have an idea about that," Maggie said, biting the end of her pencil. "Next item."

Katherine lifted a page in her notebook and studied it. "Let's see…I was thinking about having a beautification day at the park. Separate from the clearing of brush for the bridge. That will be an all-weekend job anyway. You know, maybe plant some pretty bushes or flowers, paint the trash receptacles, that sort of thing."

Maggie dropped her pencil and stared at Katherine. "What?"

"That's what I love about you. I tell you my hare-brained idea, and instead of telling me it won't work get another hobby, you embrace it and help me make it come true." She tilted her head and poked her lips out. "I love you for that."

Katherine reached her hand across the table. Maggie cupped it. "That's what friends are for," Katherine said.

"So, where were we?" Maggie said, trying to hold her emotions at bay.

"I'm going to contact the Scouts, and you're going to find a bridge helper and a sign maker."

Maggie picked up the mug of tea and sipped it. "Trey will be here in a few weeks."

Katherine lifted her brows a few times and shrugged. "I know. Are you happy? Excited?"

"Both. Nervous too."

"It's going to be okay, Maggie. I feel good about this union."

Maggie laughed. "I'm glad you feel good about it. I do too. But it's still so new and a bit strange. I've been alone for so long."

"Yes, you have, and I knew that when the perfect man came along, you'd know it. Trey is that man."

"Let's hope so. I mean, after he moves all the way out here, what if something goes wrong? Then I'll be left hiding in Eugene."

"Nothing is going to go wrong. Besides, if it does, we'll just send him packing back to San Francisco. We don't play here in Eugene, especially when it concerns our friend Maggie Regan." Katherine snapped her fingers while jerking her head.

Maggie rewarded Katherine with a happy smile mixed with a tad of uncertainty thrown in for good measure. "Glad you have my back, Katherine." She blinked a few times and then sighed wondering just how far Katherine would go in defending her honor.

CHAPTER 19

It took a few weeks to get things organized, just in time for Trey's arrival. He hit the ground running and didn't even take time to unpack the few boxes he brought. Helping Maggie with this new idea of transforming the bridge and park was hot on his list of things to accomplish. Well, that and holding her in his arms.

"Let's take a moment to breathe," he said with his arm looped over her shoulder.

She posed for a kiss. "I've been running nonstop for weeks."

Her *come get me* look led him right to her mouth. His whole body ached for her. How he could feel this much hunger for anyone was beyond him. When she ran her hands up through his hair, every inch of him tingled, intensifying the kisses. He deepened them, holding her tight against his frame, loving how she felt in his hold.

"Wow. That was so nice," she whispered.

"Uh-huh," he said, leaning back, his heart beating a mile a minute.

"I don't know how we're ever going to get any work done now that you live nearby." A Cheshire grin broadened her lips.

"I was thinking the same thing. We need distractions." He slapped at his leg. "I'll go chop some wood."

Maggie laughed. "I have plenty of wood, Trey."

"Then let's go for a walk? To the bridge?" He dug his hands into his pockets and rocked on his heels, raising his brows as he waited for her reply.

She slowly got up from the sofa. "Okay, if you insist. But I was rather enjoying your sweet kisses." She winked.

He moved to her and looped his arm around her waist. "Don't tease me, Maggie Regan." He searched her face for an answer. The answer he'd been waiting for but would never take for granted.

She pulled his arms away and took his hand. "Who's teasing?" Then she led the way down the hall.

"Mom?"

Maggie drew straight up out of bed, rolling Trey off and almost hitting the ground. "Trey. It's Collette. She's here." She jumped up, running to the mirror. She ogled her tousled hair, then ran a brush through the tangles. She stepped out of the bedroom, meeting Collette just in the hall.

"What's wrong, Mom? Are you sick?"

"No. I…I was just…taking a nap. I've been so tired with all the organizing and fund-raising." She ran her hand through her hair.

Collette's gaze went to the closed bedroom door. Then she stepped back. "I called, but you didn't answer."

"I'm sorry, hon, that you had to come all the way over to see if I was all right." She put her arm around Collette and led her to the living room. She wanted to get her as far away from the bedroom as possible.

"No worries. I was going to come by and visit anyway. Why don't you and Trey come for dinner on Saturday. We'd love to get to know him."

"That sounds good, dear. I'll ask him." She twisted a long strand of hair around her finger and rocked back on her heels.

Just then a loud thud came from the bedroom.

Collette raised her eyes over her mother's shoulder toward the bedroom. "What was that?"

"Oh nothing. Probably something fell." She put her hand on Collette's back to move her toward the front door. "I'm good. Just taking a little nap. I'll be as good as new. Thanks for coming by." She opened the door.

Collette knitted her brows together as she stepped outside. "Okay. Let me know what Trey says about dinner." She turned and took the steps down to the sidewalk level.

Maggie watched as she got into her car. She waved at her as she drove away. Then she ducked back into the house, shutting and locking the door. With her back up against the door, she cringed.

"Is she gone?" Trey asked as he peeked around the corner, his face beet red.

"Yes. I forgot to lock the door. She called. I didn't answer. She was concerned." She lowered her face and sobbed.

Trey rushed toward her. "Don't cry, hon. It's okay. She didn't see or hear anything." He rubbed her back as he tried to console her.

She raised her face and wiped the tears. "What was that loud noise?"

Trey rubbed his jawline thoughtfully, then chuckled. "Oh. That. I was trying to hear you through the wall. I accidentally knocked something off your dresser. A bottle of perfume, I think."

She shook her head and moved to the kitchen. "This episode calls for a shot of scotch." She fumbled in the cabinet and produced the bottle she'd been treasuring for months, only tasting when a situation called for a shot of courage, or to calm her nerves.

They each sipped while calming their jittery nerves. Finally, Trey spoke.

"We're adults."

"I have to ease Collette into this."

"She's an adult. She knows what adults do." He cocked his head.

"Yes, but I'm her mother."

He put the glass down and looped his hands around her waist.

"This is what got us in trouble before," she said, giving him that look again.

"I don't care who knows about us, Maggie. I love you. I'd marry you today if you'd have me, but I know you won't say yes."

She gasped. "Trey. Don't say that."

"It's true. I want to spend the rest of my life with you. I never thought I'd feel that way again, but I do. I want to wake up every morning with you by my side. I want to sit on that couch"—he pointed to the overstuffed sofa—"and stoke fires with you, drink hot tea with you…and make love to you as much—"

She rose up on her tiptoes and looped her arms around his neck, drawing him down for a kiss. He held her snug, making her feel safe while trailing kisses down her neck and back up to her mouth.

"Maggie," he mumbled in between kisses.

She could feel her pulse hammer in her wrist, her tummy doing major flip-flops, and when he eased up just a tad, she held him in place and deepened the kiss. When he stepped out of the embrace, a tug of emotion squeezed her chest. "I love you, Trey."

His eyes narrowed, and in one gentle motion, he took her in his arms and kissed her until she couldn't think, could hardly breathe, and she melted into him once more.

⁓

Her passion was strong and unashamed, and she made him want her even more. That's what he loved about her.

They quietly walked down the hall toward the bedroom. When they got halfway to the door, he stopped.

"Locked," she said, reading his mind.

He led her into the room and lifted her up onto the bed. "You are so beautiful, Maggie Regan." He moved in toward her as he watched her chest rise and fall. If only she could hear the thumping in his chest.

After they made love, she traced the line of a muscle up his arm and snuggled against his body. They fit like a glove. He'd never been this content before. Not even with Lacy. He wondered if she ever compared him to Richard.

CHAPTER 20

Just as Maggie had hoped, Collette liked Trey. Jeremy was a bit more noncommittal in his opinion, but that was typical for men judging men, or at least that's what Maggie told herself. When they had dinner together, Trey shared the portrait of Maggie with Collette. She stood admiring it for several minutes when Trey came forward and offered it to her.

"Are you serious?"

"I can paint another one. Yes, please have it with my deepest gratefulness of your love for it."

Maggie, with her arms crossed, stood in the shadows of the dimly lit kitchen as this unfolded. She had to gain her own composure before stepping in the living room, brushing a couple of stray tears away.

"I'm glad you're going to have it," Maggie said, looping her arm with Trey's.

"I'll cherish it forever." Collette brushed her hand along Trey's arm, then leaned over and kissed her mother's cheek.

⁓

The next couple of months, both of them were engaged in a lot of fund-raising. They got Collette, Jeremy, and even little Sam in on all the fun. The Scouts did their thing regarding clearing the brush, and Maggie found a wonderful man who had actually helped restore another bridge in a neighboring city, who gladly accepted her plea for help. A local artist offered to paint all the trash cans with a different scene, each depicting some aspect of the park. The covered bridge, the trees, and of course, all the wildlife.

When it came time for their first event at the park, Kathrine and Maggie worked hard. They had a couple of food trucks, a local band provided some music, and they had a donation box to help with the continued efforts of restoring the bridge and making the park a welcoming place for all.

Word got around that Maggie Regan was doing great things at Hopeberry, and people came out in droves to see. By the end of the first event, they'd received five hundred dollars in donations.

The Scouts came out for another clean-up day, and when a big truck drove up with half a dozen brand new picnic tables, Maggie shot a puzzled expression to Trey for answers. He shook his head.

When her heart regained a normal beating pattern and she could finally catch her breath, she broke down and cried.

Trey wrapped his strong arms around her and let her sob.

"Everything has been coming together so well." She laughed, trying to cheer herself up.

"And it's all because of you and Katherine that this" —he nodded beyond—"has happened."

She heaved her shoulders, and then she sighed. "It wasn't just us. Look at all the wonderful volunteers." She palmed her chest as she watched the crew put the tables in place.

"Maggie." Trey placed his hands on her shoulders and turned her to face him. "We should have a grand opening for the bridge. Let's offer to take photos and sell them, and I can set up my easel. I can offer sketches, and I'll donate all the proceeds to the Hopeberry refurbishment fund." He locked gazes with Maggie.

She threw her arms around him and gave him a big hug. "That's a perfect idea."

~

Maggie got on the computer and submitted an ad to the local newspaper office. She'd come a long way from the woman requiring help with a computer. If only the tattooed man could see her now.

Trey leaned over her shoulder and watched as she plucked away at the keyboard. He dropped a kiss on her head, then moved to her cheek. She could feel her face warm, and the tension that soon followed had her seeing cross-eyed. She whirled her chair around, and with her hands clasped in her lap, gave him that look. The one she knew got her in trouble every time. Maybe she was doing it on purpose.

"Maggie," he sang. "Don't do that. " He pulled her up and kissed her.

She leaned back and chuckled. All that did was expose her neck to him, and she already knew how much he liked to nibble his way up and to her mouth.

"Maggie, Maggie," he repeated as he trailed kisses up her neck.

"It's your fault. You came in and bothered me when

I was trying to get something done on the computer." She moved her head and let his mouth land on hers. She deepened the kiss, giving him a little taste of her teasing tongue.

He moaned softly, then picked her up in his arms and sat her on the bed. "Wait," he said, holding up a finger.

Her eyes followed him as he ran out of the bedroom and down the hall, his shoes clonking down the hardwood hall. She craned her ear. She smiled at the sound of a door locking. She crossed her legs and kept her eyes glued to the bedroom door. Soon, an out of breath Trey showed up. He ran his hand along his chin, staring her up and down. She uncrossed her legs and held out her arms. He stepped right into them and slid her back onto the bed, lowering his body on to hers. His words were slow and deliberate. Not blinking an eye, not moving a muscle he said, "Maggie. Please marry me."

"Trey. Why do you always bring this up when we're about to..." She cleared her throat.

"Because I love you that much. I don't want you to think I'm taking advantage of you."

She rose knocking him off her. "Why would I ever think that? I mean that has never even entered my mind." She stood and walked across the room and peered out the window.

"I don't know. I guess I feel I need to remind you how much I care."

"Why? Because you think I'll forget? I'm old, but I'm not senile." She refused to look at him.

"Okay. What happened to my sweet Maggie?" He rolled off the bed, making his way toward her.

She raised her shoulder to fight him off when he touched her.

"Maggie? What the heck has gotten into you?"

"Nothing. I just don't understand why you keep bringing up marriage. I think this arrangement is just fine." She crossed her arms and narrowed her eyes.

"Is it Richard?"

She cut him a foul look. "No. And don't say his name again."

He grabbed his keys off the dresser and took off out of the room. She listened for the door to close, followed by rubber hitting the road and kicking up gravel. She cupped her face and sobbed. She didn't have a clue what came over her.

~

He drove like a bat out of hell, taking the curves way too fast. What in the world just happened between them? This was so out of character for his sweet Maggie. His gaze darted left and right and straight ahead. He cranked up the music. Now blaring, it made it hard for him to think, and that's what he wanted. He ran a yellow light, then a red one, making a car screech the tires when it had to suddenly brake. Trey didn't care. More than just Maggie could act strangely.

Once inside, he sat in the dark, pondering what happened and why. Maybe it was too soon to wear his heart out on his sleeve. He'd do anything for Maggie, and he thought she felt the same way. Apparently not. Now she had pushed him away, and he'd never know what he did to make her do that. Lowering his head into his hands, he rubbed the tension from his temples.

~

Maggie called Collette, then Katherine. They both said they'd be right over. She sat in the dark living room and waited. First Collette entered.

"Mom?" She sat next to her. "What happened?"

"I don't know. We were...I said...Oh, I don't really know." She sobbed into her hands.

Just then Katherine bolted in. "Maggie, dear. What

happened?" She plopped down on the other side and slipped her arm around her.

Collette got Katherine's attention. "She's trying to tell me but is having a hard time." She raised her brows and nodded toward Maggie.

"Honey. You can tell us anything. We're here for you. What did he do?"

Maggie shot straight up. "He didn't do anything. He's always been kind and respectful. Kind of like how one would treat their parent." She grimaced.

Katherine knitted her brows. "He does not see you that way, Maggie. I've seen how he looks at you. He admires…I mean he cherishes you." She drew her mouth into a tight twist as she thought about her choice of words.

"See. You said admires. You admire your teacher, your parent. You don't admire your lover."

Collette covered her mouth to hide her gasp.

"Yes, we're doing it," Maggie said, looking straight at her daughter.

Katherine chuckled. "Now, Maggie. Let's back this up a bit. I know Trey must be devastated tonight. I can only imagine what went down here, but if you're saying these things, it makes me wonder what exactly you said to him."

"I told him to stop asking me to marry him."

Collette covered her mouth to hide her gasp. Again.

"He's asked me to marry him. More than once." She crossed her arms and pushed back into the sofa. "I just wanted things to stay the same. I was married once. To Richard. Your dad," she said, looking at Collette.

Collette reached out and touched her mom's arm. "Mom, Dad is gone. You have every right to be happy, and if marrying Trey makes you happy, then you should do it. You don't have to pretend anymore. I know you care about him. I don't have to know all the details about your um, relationship, but please, don't worry about me."

"See, Maggie. Now that's all settled you should call Trey."

"It's not all settled. I feel… I don't know. Strange about being with another person. And getting so serious."

"That's because you've been alone too darn long. Time to move on, Maggie, dear." Katherine stood. "Where's the phone?" She scouted high and low for it.

Maggie pointed behind her down the hall. Katherine made her way toward the bedroom and fetched the phone. She tossed it into Maggie's lap. "Call him. I can't tell you what to say, but you can't leave it like this. He's gotta be hurt. I know he worships the ground you walk on. I can see it in his eyes, the way he holds your gaze, the way he studies you from afar. That's true love, Maggie Regan."

"Not tonight. I can't call him now. Maybe tomorrow."

Katherine shrugged. "Suit yourself. But I think you're making a big mistake."

Collette stood. "Can I make some tea for you, Mom?"

"No, I'm going to take a long hot bath and call it a night."

"Call me in the morning," Collette said as she was leaving.

"I hope when you call him tomorrow it won't be too late." Katherine closed the door behind her.

Maggie locked the door and moseyed to the bathroom where she filled the tub full of hot water and lots of bubbles.

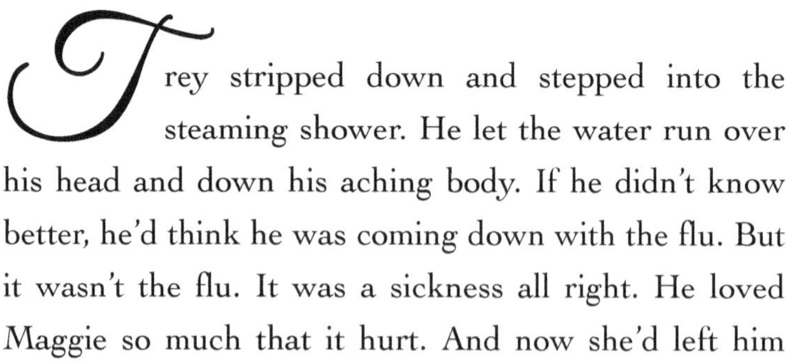

Trey stripped down and stepped into the steaming shower. He let the water run over his head and down his aching body. If he didn't know better, he'd think he was coming down with the flu. But it wasn't the flu. It was a sickness all right. He loved Maggie so much that it hurt. And now she'd left him feeling devastated, and he didn't even know what he had done.

After the hot shower, he medicated himself with whiskey, and having nothing in his stomach to absorb the alcohol, he got more than a little tipsy. He got downright drunk. He picked up his phone several times. He spoke out loud what he wanted to say. Even for him, his speech was too slurred. *Call her in the morning, jerk.* He stumbled to bed, and after just a few seconds, he fell fast asleep.

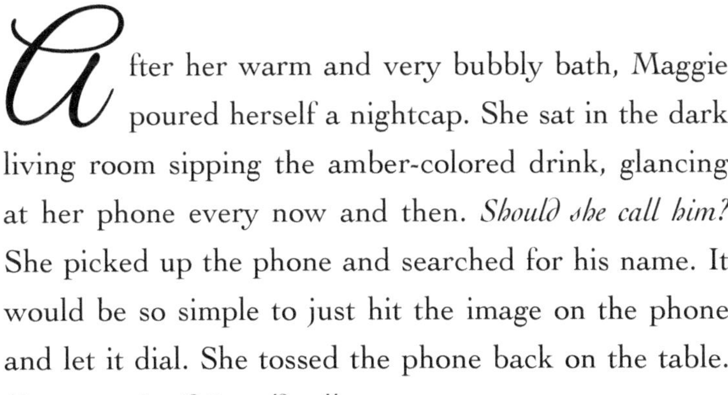

*A*fter her warm and very bubbly bath, Maggie poured herself a nightcap. She sat in the dark living room sipping the amber-colored drink, glancing at her phone every now and then. *Should she call him?* She picked up the phone and searched for his name. It would be so simple to just hit the image on the phone and let it dial. She tossed the phone back on the table. *Tomorrow. I said I would call tomorrow.*

CHAPTER 21

Tomorrow came and went, and the next day and the day after that. Every day that got further away from Maggie was one less day she could recapture Trey's interest. If he even had any, any longer.

She avoided calls from both Collette and Katherine. They were seriously blowing up her phone. The message icon indicator let her know they were also leaving messages. Or maybe it was Trey?

She listened to them one by one. No Trey. Only Collette and Katherine and two volunteers inquiring about a future event regarding Hopeberry. She sat back on the sofa, crossing her legs. Her gaze darted across the room. Dust was beginning to form on all her wood tables. She could see little dust bunnies creeping along her wood floors. She stood and made her way to the kitchen. She pulled open the cabinet doors under the sink and started hauling out cleaning supplies. Furniture polish, floor cleaner, and some lemon-scented all-purpose disinfectant for the kitchen floor. She noticed some tea spills from the table to the counter. She shook her head. Cleaning house was the last thing on her mind. She shoved all the chemicals back under the sink and got dressed. A walk. That's what she needed.

~

She went to the hall closet and pulled out a gray cable-knit sweater with deep pockets and slid her arms in. She buttoned the first couple of buttons and headed out the front door. The cool breeze of the late afternoon hit her in the face. She drew in the fresh air, smiling. Spring was just around the corner, and in fact, signs of it were already here.

She made her way to the park across the street. Not a single car parked in the lot. She picked up some litter, a candy bar wrapper, a plastic soda bottle, and a pacifier that was left behind by a toddler and tossed them into the brightly painted trash can with the birds on it. She walked further, bringing her to the newly built footbridge that would lead down the path to the bridge. She stretched her ear, listening as the creek babbled and trickled over rocks, gurgling as it made its way down to the river. She stepped up the small incline of the soft hillside and meandered down the path. Birds chirped their hello, a harmless snake trying to get a little bit of sun skedaddled when she approached, and several baby lizards rustled through the tall weeds, seeking protection. She laughed. She'd never hurt one, not on purpose anyway.

She came to the bridge but stopped before she came too close. She admired it from afar. The gleaming new white paint made it stand out. She slowly approached it, looking down every now and then to be sure she didn't step on any baby lizards, and then entered the wooden deck of the bridge. She ran her hand along the railings. The details were simple, but still so advanced for the year nineteen twenty. To think this was made by sturdy hands and no tools. Well, except the dry rot wood that needed replacing.

She leaned her back up against the railing and looked outward. A small creek ran under the bridge that connected with the first creek. The water wasn't deep, but the sides were and also rocky. The setting literally took her breath away. History, beauty, and a quiet that helped heal her soul. She lowered her head. A tear rolled down her cheek.

"A penny for your thoughts."

She wiped her face and then jerked up. "Trey?"

Trey took a few steps toward the bridge.

"What are you doing here?"

"I came to say goodbye."

She inhaled deeply before answering, letting the cool air fill her lungs. "I don't understand."

He dug his hands deep into his pockets, his eyes focused on her. "I wanted it to work out."

She gave Trey a momentary flash of regret. She tore her gaze away from the torture.

"I want you to know that nothing has changed about the way I feel for you. I thought we'd overcome most of the obstacles challenging us. But I guess I was wrong. You need to talk to a professional, Maggie. Get things straight in your head."

She turned her back on him and crossed her arms. She tried to will the tears away that were building up.

"I hope you find happiness. I really do."

She quickly wiped the tears and then whirled back around. Trey was already walking away. His pace wasn't slow and easy but fast, like he was trying to get away. She bolted down the wooden floor of the bridge and then picked up her pace down the path. Breathing hard, she called out to him. "Trey."

He stopped but didn't turn around.

"Please don't go."

He slowly eased his body around. His hand brushed over his head and settled on the back of his neck. "What?"

Maggie shuddered at his sunken eyes, his defeated tone. What had she done to him?

"I love you too. I have something to confess to you."

He took a few steps toward her. Tilting his head, he raised his brows. "Oh?"

"What I'm about to tell you, Collette doesn't even know. Only Katherine knows this. I'll tell Collette later." She hung her head.

Trey moved closer toward her. He lifted her chin with his finger. "Go on."

"I did love Richard. That is true. But what I failed to tell you was I was going to leave him the day of the tragic attack."

Trey furrowed his brows.

"I felt like I needed space. I was Richard's wife and Collette's mother. But I had no idea who Maggie was. I began to take a photography class for something to do. The instructor took an interest in me. It was strictly platonic, but he did something for me that my own husband couldn't do. He made me feel like I mattered."

"Maggie, everything I know about you and Richard tells me he did love you."

"Yes, he loved me, and I loved him. But sometimes

love isn't enough." She wiped the rolling tears away and sniffed back more.

"But how does you wanting to leave Richard have anything to do with us?"

"I felt for a long time that I was being punished for my selfishness. When Richard was taken from me and Collette, and we were on our own, it's what I had wanted, but when it happened, I was sad and devastated. I felt like I couldn't move forward, and that I had to always cherish his memory, forgoing my own happiness."

"Maggie, you never wished any harm on Richard. That I know one hundred percent. You are not to be blamed for that, just as I wasn't to be blamed for Lacy being in that elevator when she shouldn't have been."

"I still can't shake what I know. He was going to come home that night to an empty house. I had the suitcases packed. I was just waiting for Collette to get out of school."

"Where were you going to go?"

"Here. Katherine and I had discussed it. I was always headed to Eugene."

Trey grabbed Maggie by the arms. "Don't you see. No matter what, this is where you were coming. Fate. Fate brought us together."

She cocked her head. "How so? I just met you by a fluke."

He shook his head vehemently. "No, it wasn't a fluke."

She knitted her brows and then burrowed her hands in the deep pockets of her sweater.

"We were going to Eugene for our honeymoon."

"Here? Why here?" Her jaw set as she stared at him.

"We discovered the beauty of here while looking at a magazine. Then we did some more research. Lacy loved to hike, and she was determined to make me a hiker."

Maggie took her hands out of her pockets and held them out. He laced his fingers with hers.

"Please don't go. I'll go talk to someone and see if I can rid myself of the guilt so we can be a couple. I want that," she pleaded.

Lifting an interested brow, he quickly pulled her into his arms. "I love you, Maggie Regan."

"I love you too." She closed her eyes and then pulled him in for one intense kiss.

After that sweet moment, they walked hand in hand back to her house.

"How'd you know where to find me?" She held his stare.

"A little birdie told me." He dropped a kiss on her head.

"A little birdie named Katherine?"

He shook his head.

"Collette?"

"She was concerned about us. I told her I was leaving, and she begged me to come by and at least say goodbye."

"Do you think I should tell Collette about what I was going to do seventeen years ago?"

"I don't think so. What would it do? Just conjure some questions that aren't pertinent any longer. It's in the past. Keep it there."

She slid her arm around his waist. "I just don't like keeping secrets from her. I think that's why I've been such a loner."

They stopped at the park and sat at one of the picnic tables.

"Maybe when you discuss your feelings with a professional, they'll give you guidance about telling Collette or not. But for now, keep it under wraps, okay?"

She gave him a quick peck on the cheek. "Okay."

Trey knew how to lighten up any dark moment. He switched gears, causing her head to spin just a tad, but she caught up.

"I was thinking we could set up photographs for the bridge, anniversaries, engagements—" he said before she cut him off.

"Weddings?" She beamed.

"Weddings for sure." He lowered his mouth to hers and kissed her.

With his animation over the bridge and future plans, Maggie's own excitement grew for his vision. She could imagine him sketching and her shooting pictures. His passion fulfilling hers. Age was just a number. Their love was real and like the babbling brook, and the singing birds, Trey and Maggie would go on.

She patted him on the knee. "Tea?"

"I thought you'd never ask."

Hopeberry became the focal point for many photographic memories. Not only was the bridge a place for engagement and wedding photo opportunities, but the little park became the go-to place for impromptu picnics, birthday parties, and a gathering place for artists. Trey and Maggie weren't the only ones snapping pictures and sketching scenes.

During one of the warmest days when the park was hopping with families enjoying the shade trees, and some were even brave enough to dip their toes in the cold babbling creek, Trey and Maggie discussed her therapy.

"I have just a few more sessions with the doctor. You're invited to sit in on the last one. I want you there." A small smile unfolded.

"Sure. If you want me there, I'll be there." He gently knocked shoulders with her. "Can you believe how Hopeberry has transformed?"

"I know. I keep pinching myself."

"It's real, baby. It's real." He planted a kiss on her lips.

She never grew tired of how he showed his love for her. Sometimes she felt as if she'd burst from all the adoration she held in her heart for him. "Trey?"

"Uh-huh," he said, looking at dogs and kids playing.

"Is it possible to love someone too much?" She pulled his hand onto her lap and cupped it.

"Never. It's the price you pay."

She cocked her head and knitted her brows. "Price…I don't understand."

"When you love someone so much it hurts, it can devastate you beyond words if that love is ever taken from you. But if you don't love with every inch of your being, you'll never know the feeling of joy and contentment unless you do. It's the price you pay." He leaned in. "I love you so much that I can't imagine my life without you."

Her jaw relaxed, and she blinked back the tears as she tried to speak. This. This was exactly what she was feeling herself. It must be true love. "Trey, I love you so much." She leaned in. Their mouths just mere centimeters apart, she posed for the kiss. "I can't lose you. Ever." She moved in, her bottom lip mingling with his top lip. She closed her eyes and drank in the moment, wishing it would never end. Just then a ball plopped right into their lap, startling them both.

"Sorry, lady," a little boy said, grabbing his ball and running away.

Trey and Maggie laughed so hard they were crying.

"I guess someone is telling us something." He pulled her up off the bench.

With her camera dangling from the wide black strap around her neck, and him lugging his easel and case with paints, the two headed back toward the house. But not for hot tea. No. Iced tea to quench their thirst on this very warm summer day.

~

They held hands during the entire one-hour appointment. The doctor did most of the talking, informing Trey of all the strides they'd made, and how Maggie wanted to move forward.

"Maggie's come to terms with what happened

regarding Richard and his death. She also realizes that although she was considering leaving him, we don't know for sure if she would have gone through with it. True, she had suitcases packed, but she could have left many times before. Those suitcases were packed for over thirty days."

Trey grunted. "I didn't know that." He squeezed Maggie's hand.

"I forgot that part. I guess I tucked it so far back into my memory I couldn't retrieve it."

"We've talked at length, and some of it I can't divulge because of patient-doctor privilege, but she did want you to know that part." The doctor read over her notes before continuing. "So, this is our last appointment. But if at any time you feel the need to talk about anything, I'll be happy to see you. I hope you two have a wonderful life together. You deserve it. Both of you."

❧

Over lattes and cookies at their favorite little café, Trey and Maggie didn't talk about the meeting. No, instead they talked about how they were going to move forward in their relationship.

"Nothing has changed, Maggie." He held her hand

tight on top of the table, and with his free hand, held his coffee.

She tilted her head. "What do you mean?" She pulled her mouth into a twisted knot.

"I want to marry you."

She pulled her head back and laughed. "Oh, that." She lowered her eyes, focusing on his sparkling eyes and handsome face.

"Well?"

She tipped her chin twice.

He bolted out of the chair and ran around to her side, taking her face into his hands. "Seriously? You're saying yes?"

"Under one condition." She pursed her lips tightly.

"Anything." He knelt down on bended knee.

"We get married on the bridge with Collette, Jeremy, Sam, and Katherine as witnesses."

"I have one better. We invite my parents, and a few friends— and I want it to take place in the fall. The same time I first laid eyes on you. I want the leaves to be red and gold, with just a little chill in the air. I want to replay the day I met you."

Maggie detected misting in Trey's eyes. She palmed her heart, and then tears began to form. She swallowed hard before she spoke. Choking back all the raw emotion she'd been holding on to, she managed to squeak out, "You've made me so happy." She offered her hands to him.

He laced his fingers with hers. "We're going to be great together, Maggie Regan. Just wait and see." A genuine smile spread across his lips, making her all warm inside. She squeezed his hand and nodded. "I know we will be. And yes, I do believe."

He cocked his head, furrowing his brows. "Believe?"

"I believe we were always destined to be together. How it all came about, we have no control over, but I'm at peace and feel I can be truly happy now."

"Me too. Talk about coming full circle." He stood, pulling her up with him. "How about we get out of here?" He winked, setting her cheeks on fire.

"I thought you'd never ask." She looped her arm around his waist, and the two exited the small café with a twinkle in their eyes, a light in their step, and lots of love in their heart.

The next book in this stand-alone series is Florida Fling. Enjoy!

Debbie

ABOUT THE AUTHOR

A USA Today bestselling author, Debbie writes sweet contemporary romance and women's fiction. She currently lives on the east coast with her husband. She loves to hike, work in the garden, and on most sunny days you can find her enjoying her backyard. She's an avid supporter of animal rescue, and as such, pledges to happily donate a percentage of all book sales to local and national rescue organizations. When you purchase any of her books, you're also helping animals.

To find out more about Debbie, check out her website at https://www.authordebbiewhite.com

Perfect Pitch

Ties That Bind

Passport To Happiness

The Missing Ingredient

The Salty Dog

The Pet Palace

Billionaire Auction

Billionaire's Dilemma

Coaching the Sub

Christmas Romance – Short Stories

9 781955 315081